NO BODY NO CRIME

RAY TOUGH

To my wife, Angie, for giving me the encouragement, inspiration and patience that has allowed me to complete this book.
I love her dearly…

Corpus Delicti
The foundation or material substance of a crime.
The phrase Corpus Delicti might be used to mean the
physical object upon which the crime was committed, such
as a dead body or the charred remains of a house, or it
might signify the act itself, that is, the murder or arson.
What it does not mean is No Body, No Crime

PROLOGUE

In the British prison system there has never been a "Death Row".

It was a cell, usually in very close proximity to the execution shed.

The only method of judicial execution, for many centuries, had been by hanging.

It was in such a place, in June 1949, that three people sat.

Two of them were prison officers whilst the other was a man under sentence of death.

This man's name was Nicholas Jenkins, although since his arrest, and trial, some newspapers had given him the sobriquet of "The Oil Drum Murderer".

The name stuck and it always would…

There were no windows for natural light and no clock. The officers came and went according to their shift patterns but they were there all the time he was, 24 hours a day.

Jenkins had been convicted of the murder of a 69-year-old widow, Mrs Amelia Sanders, but in reality, he had murdered five other people. Although not charged with these deaths, as was common practice then, the details became part of the prosecution case. These killings were quite horrendous; after their deaths, he had disposed of their bodies using sulphuric acid. He then lived off the profits of their estates

Some of the worst, if not the worst, the Police had ever come across.

Jenkins sat at a metal-topped table on a seat that resembled a folding garden chair; he was writing a letter. The letter would be given to his solicitor together with the "memoirs" he had been writing with the permission of the authorities for the past few weeks.

The officers supplied cups of tea, cigarettes and sharpened his pencils.

The task he had set himself was over, as his life nearly was.

He asked for a cigarette, which was lit for him.

Tomorrow he would change into his smart green suit that he had last worn at the Assizes.

It would be his last day on earth...

Chapter 1

ALMOST EXACTLY A YEAR AGO, in May 1967, as I was sitting having my usual breakfast of toast and coffee, the doorbell to my flat rang.

As far as I knew, I was not expecting anyone and certainly not at 8.30 in the morning.

I lived in a block of six purpose-built flats spread over two floors built in the 1950s. From the outside, its shape was rectangular and surrounded by communal gardens.

All the residents had a car parking space allotted to them for those that had cars, that is.

It was just outside the city centre of Chichester, where I had always lived, but I had lived in this particular flat, on the first floor, since my last surviving parent, my father, had died ten years earlier.

I went down the stairs and opened the front door via the lobby. At the door was our regular postman.

"Something for you Mr Dean, that has to be signed for." I signed his pad and took possession of a bulky, manila envelope addressed to:

Mr Max Dean,

Flat 6, Southleigh Gardens,
Chichester,
Sussex.

It was securely taped all round with clear sticky tape. I looked at the postmark stamped "Alnwick".

The question was, who did I know in Alnwick? I didn't even know where it was!

I retraced my steps to the flat and went back in, closing the door behind me. I put the kettle on to make some fresh coffee still clutching this envelope in my left hand.

Coffee made, I sat at my desk in the smaller of the two bedrooms that I had converted into a study containing the desk, with a portable typewriter, and a chair.

I took off the tape and opened the letter itself using a letter opener.

I emptied the contents onto the now empty desk top. What grabbed my attention first was a sealed, much smaller envelope addressed to "Max".

I was even more intrigued, if that was possible.

This, whatever it was, was intended for me, there was no doubt about that.

Using my letter opener again, I slit it open and found it contained a handwritten letter:

17 George Street
Amble, Northumberland.
Telephone: Amble 8340
Date as postmark

Dear Cousin Max,
I hope that this letter finds you well, as I am. I am sorry that it has taken a long time to contact you.
This manuscript has been written by Nick Jenkins, I am sure that you remember him! And the envelope it came in originally was addressed to

my parents. Written across it in my father's handwriting were the words, "Never show her this" in thick black ink. I came across it a few years ago when I was clearing out their house after they were both dead. I have read bits of it, since I came across it, but I cannot bring myself to read all of it.

It would be too upsetting, even after all these years.

Good God, Nick Jenkins. One of the most infamous murderers this country has ever had. He was known as "The Oil Drum Murderer". He had murdered six people then immersed their bodies in acid. It was horrific.

Veronica, my cousin and the author of this letter, had been his "Lady Friend", for want of a better expression, from a young age and had given evidence at his trial. A trial I had attended to give her some moral support. After the trial was over, Veronica literally disappeared off the face of the earth. No one had seen her and she hadn't been in touch with me, until this letter that is.

I continued reading …

It will take you a while to read, but it is by him. I had enough letters from him so I recognise the handwriting. Is it true? Some of it will be, but who knows about the rest? That sounds like a description of him doesn't it. A life built on lies, lies and death.

Maybe, in a perverse way, he is trying to tell the "proper" story. I don't know. What you do with it is up to you, I never want to see it again, but you might find it of interest. I am sorry if this has come as a bit of a shock to you.

It would be good to hear from you, please write or telephone me. Cousin Veronica.

Chapter 2

MAX DEAN IS my name and I am a reporter on the local paper, the Chichester Times. I cover trials at Lewes Assizes, appearances at Chichester Magistrates Court, and anything to do with crime.

I was born in Chichester in 1920 and went to the local grammar school where I developed a love of the English language. I like to think that I still have it.

I was an only child; mum was a homemaker and dad worked as a draughtsman in an engineering factory that made parts for aircraft. Work that would later excuse him from the call up after the outbreak of the War.

I have always been keen on sport and played football to a reasonable standard. To this day, I still support Brighton but they are languishing in Division 3.

It was almost preordained that I would go to university, which was almost unheard of then. Mum and dad were very supportive and made huge sacrifices.

I went to Reading where I read English. I worked hard and earned a good degree. (A First) I met some lifelong friends, some of whom would lose their lives in the conflict that started in September 1939.

Whilst I was studying, the government introduced conscription for all able-bodied men between the ages of 18 to 41. I could have deferred my course but chose to finish it. Anyway, the war might be over by the time I had finished. I had worked too long and too hard and might never get the opportunity again.

An informal graduation ceremony took place back home to say my goodbyes to my parents and then I left for Aldershot for basic Army training, as my call up papers had been ready for a while. I had not been at all ready for what was to come. I had actually chosen the Royal Air Force, but the Army was short of manpower, so the Army it was.

I hated every minute of it. Square bashing, being sworn and shouted at and totally depersonalised. The upsides, and there were some, were I made some good mates and achieved a level of physical fitness that I have never managed to get back to.

We always seemed to be hungry so food parcels from home were a Godsend and we shared with those less fortunate. We were all in it together. Towards the end of these ten weeks of "hell", the pressure on us eased a lot.

I had many new skills under my belt including being able to march in time and how to kill people. We began to be allocated regiments and I was posted to the Intelligence Corps. I was pleasantly surprised; it could have been a lot worse.

I was given leave for ten days and told to report for duty to Winchester, in Hampshire, where my induction with the Intelligence Corps began. I was treated like a human being and thought that there must be a catch; there wasn't one, not then, not ever.

There, my story of what I did in the war has to end, not because I do not want to share it, but because I am not allowed to. Except to say, that I rose to the dizzy heights of being a Corporal. Because of what I did, I am bound by the Official Secrets Act; it is not up for debate or discussion, it's a law that I have to abide by and probably always will have to.

Chapter 3

I MADE myself a cup of tea and started to read what Veronica had posted to me. I don't know why I was surprised, but it seemed to be really well written. The spelling and grammar were commendable. Journalists, and teachers, are very fussy when it comes to these things.

I WAS BORN on the 15ᵗʰ February 1908 in Leeds and my given name Nicholas was an homage to the then Czar of Russia, Nicholas the second. I will die on the 2ⁿᵈ June 1949 at precisely 9am. If that sounds dramatic then so be it. Please indulge me, this is my story, my life as I wish to tell it. I am not sure whether anyone will ever read it, especially Veronica, but perhaps her parents will pass it on. On the other hand, if they want to burn it they can do that.

(Veronica, you will never know how much you meant to me and I truly hope that you find happiness and that it is long lasting)

My mother and father, Margaret and Harold, were quite old when I came along. Mother was 37 years old and father being 41 years of age. Looking back they always seemed to me to be old people, certainly when compared to the parents of the few friends that I had or was allowed to have. Father, I always referred to him as that, worked in an office in a tailoring factory and mother was a seamstress at the same place. It was where they met. After my birth, mother gave up work and money, which had never been abundant, became even scarcer.

We lived in a "two up, two down" terraced house off Beckett Street in the Burmantofts area of Leeds, it was just outside of the city centre. An outside toilet was normal, and of course still is for a lot of people. No garden of course, no hot water, it had to be heated with a gas geyser in the kitchen, such as it was. Coins of various denominations would be inserted into a slot in the gas meter. Bath night, once a week on a Friday, was a tin bath in front of the fire. As a child, even in the summer, it always seemed to be a cold house and I had a succession of childhood illnesses. I didn't know the difference but looking back, it was awful.

If you do read this Veronica, much of what you read will be new to you as during my years with you I told you so many lies. I felt that I had to maintain our relationship and for that please forgive me, not that I expect you ever would. It would be naïve to think that. I will not refer to you again by name as I do not wish to upset you any more than I already have done.

My first school was just around the corner from where we lived, I think I enjoyed it but can't really remember. What I can remember is that I was isolated from the other children in the street, not totally, but enough not to have proper friends. I never had bikes, a football, or even scooters to play on. The others seemed to be allowed to play out longer than me as well. My "tea" would be ready before they were called in. Mother always encouraged me to read and write and father gave me spelling tests and times tables tests .We read the bible every evening and I always said my prayers. Weekly, and sometimes twice weekly, we, as a family, would travel to our place of worship; it wasn't a church, just an austere building. We would sit amongst other people in total silence. I was told, when I asked, that the purpose was to wait for God. I didn't know the difference. I thought it was normal but it did give me a head start looking back. I gained a scholarship to the local grammar school at the age of eleven. It was two tram rides away in the north of the city. I loved tram journeys. I spent the next four years at this school and whilst there my "real talents" were developed. I used to call it copying, the Police called it forgery, which of course is what it was.

I seemed to have a talent for copying, if talent be the correct word. It will have to do, I have little time to get involved in semantics. I think it started in an art class when we were studying "Old Masters", really we did, photographs of them in books of course. I started to imitate the signatures of Rembrandt, Canaletto and the like. To my young eyes they were rather good facsimiles. It snowballed from there.

I was "copying" end of term school reports, making "bad" or "mediocre" into "good" for some of my classmates who would pay me quite well. Realising the potential, I obtained a supply of blank report books from an unlocked stock cupboard.

I would take this "work" home with me and each one took a long while to complete; it was only done a few times a year though, at the end of each term. I made friends this way and the payment was usually cigarettes or sweets. As an aside I gave up sweets but not cigarettes.

I was caught, just the once, practising a teacher's signature on a piece of paper on my desk. I managed to talk myself out of trouble; he was a relatively new teacher and I like to think that I wound him around my little finger.

I forget now what I said but it must have been plausible enough to be believed. He wasn't senior enough to write end of term reports.

I am trying to write this account of my life in some sort of chronological order but from time to time I may well write out of sequence.

You may well be wondering how this manuscript, that does sound rather grand doesn't it, got out, so to speak. The answer is quite simple; I was allowed writing materials and it was done with the permission of Mr Dixon, the Governor. It has kept me occupied and for that, I suppose my guards, the prison officers, should be grateful. I have never given them a minute's trouble. So no scandals here; no wrongdoing by the officers. I will give it to my solicitor and he will do the rest. I am not being paid for this and even if I was, it would do me no good. But speaking of being paid, and as I said some of this is out of sequence, let me put the record straight regarding the News of the World.

When I was arrested and news of what I had done began to filter through, no doubt from poorly paid police officers eager to supplement their incomes, I was contacted through my solicitor on a series of handwritten notes by just about every Sunday newspaper. They all wanted to serialise my story in print in exchange for them paying for my defence. It wasn't a hard choice to make. Although I despised the News of the World, I went with them. Think about it if you will, millions and millions of people reading about me and I would have the very best defence that money could buy. I would certainly need it, although it came to naught as I fully expected it would.

At school I developed a lifelong interest in music; we had a very good music master, a Mr Holt if memory serves. I learned to play the piano and my parents, who had moved to one of the better suburbs by now, bought an upright piano. I practised and practised. Father had been promoted and mother carried out alteration work at home on her sewing machine. I could now walk to school and I did. I carried on "copying" as and when my services were required. I like to think that I had a hand in them being successful in the start of their working lives as school reports were always looked at by potential employers. I never had the need to use the technique on any of my reports, which always struck me as being somewhat ironic. One of the many, many ironies in my life.

I, like the rest of the country, was well aware of what

Jenkins had done and I suppose he paid the price. I did not cover the trial. (I have already mentioned that I travelled to Leeds whilst it was taking place, to be with my cousin). The nationals did that. I remember that the News of the World actually serialised his story.

I was getting a feel for him and it wasn't a good feeling. What an egotistical, arrogant man, "millions of people reading about him". It was true, millions of people did read about him, week by week and I was no exception. It was the talk of the land, but anything to do with murders and trials usually was.

I thought back then, to when the story first broke…

Our newsroom, in common with other local newspapers up and down the country, had a teletype machine installed so we could keep abreast of news a bit further afield. We had news from both Reuters and the Press Agency. We had all the national daily and Sunday papers as well.

Back in January 1949, as I was about to leave the office to have a pint at our local" watering hole", which was almost next door to us, there was a huddle gathering around the wireless to listen to the 5 o'clock news. By the time I walked over this little crowd had dispersed. Our editor, Tom Hourigan, took his unlit pipe out of his mouth and said, "Blimey lads, that's a hell of a story, but it's miles away and of no interest to us, and the big boys will cover that anyway."

Because I had missed hearing it, I asked him to precis it for me. "A man has appeared at court in Leeds charged with murdering an old lady. He put her body in a tub of acid, bloody acid! Would you believe it?"

It became the talk of the office and we continued talking about it in the pub. When I got home, my dad was full of it too and with good reason.

He had had a letter from his brother Douglas in Leeds telling him that my cousin Veronica had been seeing this man, this alleged murderer, for quite a few years and he knew him too. He had rented the place the killings took place at to him...

Chapter 4

AT THE END of 1945 the door to "Civvy Street" beckoned, I knocked long and hard but it took a while to open. What could I do? What was I equipped to do as a demobbed Corporal from the Intelligence Corps? I wanted to be a reporter, a journalist. It was as simple as that.

I wrote to every newspaper that I could think of, offering my "services" as a reporter but without an ounce of experience. I waited for the twice a day post, but got nothing, nothing at all; or if a reply came, it was a variation on a theme. Thanks but no thanks, no experience etc. etc.

I wasn't penniless, I had saved some money from the Army and mum and dad were very good. But I was getting more and more despondent; rejection wasn't a word that I was used to. I even considered joining up again…

1945 turned into 1946, I still kept in touch with friends from University and from the Army, most of whom had jobs. One of them asked if I had contacted the local paper. Such was my rush to get into Fleet Street, that I hadn't even considered it, I don't know why.

The Chichester Gazette had been around a long time so off I went, cap in hand, and knocked on its door. In the Army I had learned to type and had learned shorthand, at my own expense, as I thought that one day it might be useful. That day, it transpired, had just dawned. The editor seemed to be impressed, after I had made an appointment to see him, and I was set on as a junior reporter. I was given a three month trial period.

26 years of age and a junior reporter but the salary, or weekly wage as it was, was not a lot of money. It would improve though in time. It wasn't until many years later that I found out that the editor was a distant relative of my dad. It was a nepotistic business. Dad didn't think to mention it, but he was like that.

I was asked to look at births, weddings and funerals or "Hatches, Matches and Despatches" as it was called in the profession I had just joined.

The area around Chichester is a lovely part of the world and fairly affluent too. Social events were always well attended, especially christenings, weddings and even funerals. There was always something to report on. I got to know the ropes and the staff especially, and got a permanent position and the pay rise I had been promised. Although a weekly publication we still had deadlines to adhere to and I loved the challenges that it brought. It wasn't, by any means, a Monday to Friday 9 to 5 job.

On the Gazette we had two excellent photographers (Smudgers). They covered every event worth taking photos of from the action on the pitch in the football season at Brighton and Hove Albion to Society weddings in and around our circulation area. As good as they were, they weren't mind readers, they needed to be pre-booked for events that I was reporting on. A mistake I only made the once when I forgot to book one of them and the efforts from my Box Brownie only just made it into the paper. I was mildly chastised over a pint, but I got away with it with no real harm done. I was learning my craft.

On a personal level I had a series of relationships, but they didn't last. Mainly they were young women I had met either whilst out on a job or at social gatherings that the cricket and golf clubs held. I played neither, but they were social hubs. Trips to the cinema and drinks in country pubs were the extent of my romances. I was all right with it; my mum and dad were not. Grandchildren were expected to be part of their lives as they got older. It was an expectation that never materialised. I never married, although I have girlfriends from time to time; no strings, no ties; it suits me.

At the paper, the newsroom was always a busy place and one of my close friends worked on the crime "beat". He covered everything from liaising with the local boys in blue for gossip, the Magistrates and Coroners' Courts and sometimes, further afield, he would go to Lewes Assizes if there was a trial with local interest taking place.

On one occasion I went with him to cover a trial there in my own time. On this visit, a man was on trial for attempted murder.

The accused was a recently retired British Army soldier; he had been a sergeant. It was alleged, that he had shot the lover of his wife of more than ten years. He had caught them together, in their house, after his suspicions had been aroused. He had used a Webley service revolver that he had acquired during the war, Army issued, but not to him as an NCO, and shot the man in the head at very close range. The man, now classified as the victim, survived thanks to the skill of the surgeons who saved his life. He came into the court in a wheelchair that he would need for the rest of his life. He was not in a good way at all.

There would be no trial as such, the former soldier had pleaded guilty, but the proceedings were still like a drama, a drama without a script for the actors. The man in the dock presented as a sorry sight, badly dressed and to my untrained eyes he looked to be "not quite with it". A stark contrast to the bewigged orators, one asking for the key to be thrown away and the other, his defence counsel, asking for medical help for his client.

He was sentenced to fifteen years with hard labour and for good measure the Judge said to him, "And when you are released, turn your life around. The war is over, you can't go around shooting people anymore." I was lost for words but entranced, in a perverse way, at what I had just witnessed.

On our way back I volunteered my services to my colleague to cover his beat when he was on holiday or unavailable. He thought I must be mad, I thought, "but not as mad as that man in the dock". The editor agreed without hesitation, and without the fight I had half expected. That was the start of my unrequited love affair with crime.

I did enjoy it, it had its boring moments of course, but overall it was more interesting than the weddings and social events that I usually covered. It was a foot in the door.

My colleague eventually retired and I was promoted. When my "bylines" were printed it said, "Crime Reporter" under my name. It was very pleasing from a professional point of view and when I went out with my parents, they never failed to name drop as if I was someone famous. It pleased them and caused me some little embarrassment, sometimes.

I have to say, without "blowing my own trumpet", that I built up a reputation for reporting what actually went on inside the courts or police stations rather than what I wanted the public to read from any sort of sensational angle. I left that to the Sunday papers.

Maybe that is one of the reasons that Fleet Street never came knocking at my door, who knows? I covered many major trials at the Assizes at Lewes.

Chapter 5

Now for a job. I had a School Certificate, a real one, not a copy! And I was ready to start work. It was 1923 and thanks to the War the world was a very different place. There was a huge choice as a school leaver, but conventional apprenticeships didn't interest me at all. I wasn't going to get my hands dirty if I could help it. An office job of some sort then, something with long-term prospects. Through a contact of father an interview was arranged at a firm of solicitors, irony or fate, take your pick. I got the job as an office junior and started almost at once.

The hours were 8.30am until 5pm Monday to Friday and Saturdays from 9am until 12noon. I was excited at having my own money in my pocket. I had worked out that after paying for my tram tickets I would be left with four shillings. My mother made me sandwiches wrapped in brown paper and tied with string, just like she had done when I was at school, and a piece of fruit every day.

I was kept busy and my job to start with was just doing what I was told, delivering documents to other solicitors' offices and even barristers' chambers. The practice in Park Square, Leeds, was a mixed practice and as such dealt with civil and criminal law. I didn't know there were different types of law, but I was a quick learner. I was complimented on my appearance and this stuck with me for the rest of my life, although for different reasons. I had few friends and although I liked female company I didn't really go out with many. Occasionally, three or four of us would take in the latest Variety shows at the Leeds Empire or somewhere similar, a half of bitter, which I never really took to, after the show then home.

As the years went by I was doing well at the office and had been assisting articled clerks in preparing conveyancing for house sales and purchases and will writing. My handwriting was complimented upon and I was steadily advancing up the ladder that would only ever allow me to be a clerk. I was bored, it was dull work and I thought I needed some excitement. I thought about actually joining the Army but decided that it was too dangerous, peacetime or not. Being killed for King and Country was not for me. Father talked me out of it, he had avoided the call up in the War due to his age.

I HAD TO PAUSE, as I had to every now and again, to absorb what I was reading, but looking at the amount, there was an awful lot more to read. Pages and pages of it, was it true? Was it accurate? So far, apart from his foray into what he euphemistically called "copying" there was not a hint of any real criminal actions. And what did he mean about "waiting for God?"

Questions; questions, that could never be answered. That would remain the most common theme throughout. When and how did it start to go wrong? I put the kettle on, not for the first or certainly last time, emptied the overflowing ashtray, made some coffee, had a rest and then picked up where I had left it…

Don't ask me why, but I started taking home legal documents from the practice. Blank conveyance documents, blank Wills and Power of Attorney forms that would become my favourites much later. They were standard forms used throughout the country with nothing to identify the practice. That was usually done with a wax seal. I had already got the use of a typewriter at home; it belonged to father but he never used it. I practised over and over again. I made up names and amounts for the Wills. I saw these on a daily basis in the office and my efforts looked just as good. I can honestly say though I didn't have a plan that involved any form of dishonest, although it must have remained in my subconscious.

Started taking home legal documents? What on earth for? Who does that? The seed was well and truly planted then. Rhetorically I asked, who does he think he is kidding? More questions and answers that I would never get…

I took home letters from the office from clients to practise my handwriting skills and get used to the terminology involved. I didn't understand a lot of it but I didn't need to.
All of what I copied was put on the fire and the letters returned without anyone knowing. Eventually I decided that my time was up in the world of clerking. The pay wasn't very good and I felt undervalued; time for a change, but just before I changed jobs let me explain about the little Latin phrase that got me where I am today. Corpus Delicti.
Thanks to me everyone in the whole country knows what it means now! Or if they read the News of the World they should do! I mentioned that from time to time I worked in the "crime" side of the practice. On one occasion I wrote the phrase down and curiosity got the better of me, I had never come across it before, so I asked a senior clerk what it meant.
He shouted over from where he was sitting, with his usual cigarette in the corner of his mouth, "If you don't have a body, you don't have a crime". The explanation stuck but looking back two things stand out:
He was having a joke at my expense or
He genuinely believed it too.

Another irony is that it took until I was interviewed by the Police to find out what it really meant, and of course by that time it was far too late wasn't it?

I needed a car and wanted better clothes to wear. I had seen an advertisement for trainee salesmen at a car showroom in the city centre in the evening paper. I got the job and said my goodbyes to the Solicitors, but not before taking home lots of blank forms, for a rainy day. I was paid on commission with a small basic salary. I did all right though and managed to buy a small car through the motor trade. It was now 1932, I was 23 years of age and at last, according to father and mother, there was a young lady in my life. She was called Angela. We met in the queue at the Hyde Park Cinema; it was raining and I offered her my umbrella. We started to walk out with each other and went for tea and walks. We were getting along swimmingly, so swimmingly in fact that she informed me that she was carrying my child! This, to say the least, came as a complete shock to me although I did know how babies were made. I just couldn't contemplate what would be expected, save to say that it probably involved marriage. She told me that she was about three months pregnant and it been confirmed by a doctor. I believed her but I had heard stories of men being "trapped" by women into marriage when there was no baby.

I would do the right thing and marry her. We informed our respective parents, although I never met hers, ever, who were not best pleased. We married at the Register Office and had a hurried three day honeymoon in Scarborough which I could barely afford. She was a waitress and had no savings or money behind her. We moved into a rented house that was like going back to my early childhood, it was awful. Father and mother helped out with buying us second hand furniture and the like. It was not too far away from where I worked but I drove to work, it was the only car in the street.

(Most of the sales at the showroom were by finance deals, it was called Hire Purchase, "never, never" to use the vernacular. It was very popular as it allowed people, for a small deposit, to buy a new car then pay for it until all the payments, subject to an addition of

interest, were made. It would then become the property of the owner; until then the car belonged to the finance company.)

We were paid commission by the Finance people too, but the senior salesmen got the best deals. As ever in my life, I wanted more.

Then the baby arrived and my world changed. I was not cut out for fatherhood at all. After a week in hospital she brought the child home; I did visit once or twice and the baby looked fine, my parents doted on her, I never did.

The marriage fell apart shortly after the birth of the baby girl that my wife called Bernadette. I couldn't cope with the crying from the baby and I couldn't cope with my wife. She was lazy and couldn't cook. She left, taking the baby with her and to this day I have no idea what happened to them. I never even met her parents as they didn't come to the wedding and I never got a divorce so I suppose I am still legally married. No suppose in the eyes of the Law, I am still married.

I was relatively busy at the showroom. But not busy enough, not enough money coming in for my liking. On a whim I decided to start up on my own selling second hand cars. I had built up quite a few contacts in the motor trade and worked from home with the cars either parked outside or at my parents. I always had a stock of two or three. I advertised in the Yorkshire Evening News and it was a cash only business. The first one I sold made me a profit of £35.00, not a fortune but a start. I needed some premises but to do that I would need more money than I had. After a few months of sales I went to see my bank manager to ask for a business loan. I was full of confidence, the bank manager wasn't. "Come back in three years", he said. Three years? I had been chastised by a little man in a striped suit who couldn't see further than the end of his nose. I came out of his office bitter and angry although I never got angry. My life had to change and change it did, but not for the better.

In a nutshell, I started selling cars and arranging finance for people who didn't exist. It didn't take long for this little scheme to unravel. The hire purchase companies wrote to these "people" and not getting a reply came straight to my door. I was arrested, interviewed and summonsed to appear at the Magistrates Court. I was eventually sentenced to 18 months, of which I served just over a year. My mother and father were devastated. It was a harrowing experience for me and them to say the least. I did not enjoy my time in prison at all and really should have learned from the experience.

I had asked father and mother not to visit me and they didn't, but at the gate of Leeds prison on my release date was my father. He drove me home in silence. I was back home, 26 years old, penniless with no prospects.

A job in a newsagents was next, he was a friend of my father. Up at dawn to take in the newspapers and number them for the delivery boys to deliver. I had a break at lunchtime then back in time for the teatime papers to be delivered and dealt with in the same way. On a Sunday we only had the morning papers to be delivered so we closed at lunchtime. I did quite enjoy it although it was mundane and the early starts did me no good at all. The shop had a stocktake every six months when the owner discovered that stocks of my favourite brand of cigarettes did not tally with sales. I didn't have the chance to either explain or to protest my innocence. The shopkeeper was no fool. He sacked me on the spot and informed my father who at once made good the financial shortfall. I became the talk of the neighbours, all of whom used the newsagents on a daily basis.

So back to square one again. I really had no idea what to do. If it was crime I would not get caught, that much I was sure of. I seemed to have little choice.

Chapter 6

I WAS ALWAYS QUITE *a gregarious person and made friends easily. As I got older, these friends were, in actual fact, people that I could use for one reason or another. I "saved" them in the back of my mind, or wrote the names down in a little book. I had made a few contacts in prison. I didn't associate with burglars or anyone who used violence, I suppose they were nearly all what you would call "con men", confidence tricksters of all kinds. Pleasant people to while away the hours inside with, but not too bright, some of them. I had mentioned, more than once, that I thought I was pretty good at copying documents. I did it to improve my standing in the hierarchy in prison.*

I did share my parents' telephone number with one or two inside and unexpectedly I got a call from one of them. It was William Flynn, always William, never Bill or Billy. He wanted to meet up to discuss a business proposition. We arranged to see each other in a café in Leeds city centre. This business proposition involved me doing what I did best i.e. forgery. William used the term and so did I from then on. Forging some house documents, as he called them, so that he could sell the house his mother lived in. When he explained what it involved it made sense or rather the £200 cash he promised me made sense. I still had my blank conveyancing forms that I had hidden in the loft at home years before. The rainy day had arrived. We would need a short term let that we could use as an office and William would fund this. He was aware that his mother, who he had said he didn't get on with, was travelling to Devon to look after her elderly sister and would be away for at least three months. What he wasn't aware of, as he rarely saw his mother, was that she had a new next door neighbour, in the adjoining semi-detached house, and he was, of all things, a retired Detective Sergeant.

She had asked him to keep an eye on the property and he did just that; he prevented the house from being sold from under her. How, you may well wonder?

William was in the process of showing two prospective purchasers around early one evening, he had always had a set of keys. He turned up in his car and the two "buyers" turned up in a small laundry van with the name of the company on the sides of it together with a telephone number. The neighbour watched what was going on through the upstairs bedroom window and heard movement next door. He made a note of the registration numbers and the name of the laundry. Once a copper always a copper eh? The people left. He had never met William, but was aware of his existence through his mother. He phoned the local police station and spoke to a former colleague.

I was oblivious to all this of course; I was working hard on some of the documents and in the process of renting a bogus office for our fictitious solicitor to work from. The knock on the door said it all, three police officers, one Detective Constable and two in uniform. The paperwork was in front of me on the table! William had been arrested for attempted fraud and had sung like a canary.

Instead of the £200 I was promised I got four years in prison, William received a five-year sentence.

My "Alma Mater" this time was H.M.P Lincoln. I knew how to behave in prison, I was almost an "old lag". After a few weeks I got a job in the tinsmith's shop, it was that or the laundry and I thought it might be more interesting. We used hand tools, solder and sulphuric acid for cleaning the joints of the tin trays we made for the bakery trade. Whilst daydreaming one day I saw a mouse run in front of me on the shop floor. I was bored so I tried to catch it, threw an oily rag over it and then stood on it. In a flash I wondered if the acid I used on a daily basis would dissolve the mouse. I put the dead rodent into a glass jar and poured acid over it. I hid it in a corner out of sight. I was quite excited at what I might find the next day, my mind was working overtime for reasons that by now you will know all about.

All that was left the next day was a brown sludge. I stirred the contents with a piece of wood and there was nothing left of the mouse. I actually paid my inmate friends with cigarettes to provide me with more specimens.

I shared my "discovery" with some of my prison friends and also shared with them my "Corpus Delicti" theory. I genuinely thought that I had discovered the basis of the "perfect crime".

It was so simple, find a rich victim, kill them somehow, dissolve their bodies in acid, pour it away then sell their house and car and reap the rewards. Of course it would take a lot more acid, but that didn't seem to present a problem. It was all I thought about. No body, no crime, no crime no court appearance, why had no one thought about it before?

We had been at War since September 1939 and rumours and facts circulated about "conscription" which was the "forced" entry into the armed services for men between certain ages. You had no choice in the matter unless you were in a restricted occupation or mentally incapable. Being in prison I was safe for the time being. When I was released, however, it was a different matter, it was the old "King and Country" thing again. I was discharged with no one at the gates this time and caught the train back to Leeds. I had a job to go to, but not in the accepted sense; it was via some of my new-found "friends" and it involved a new venture that became known as the "Black Market", it seemed to be right up my street, as long as I didn't get caught that is.

I used the family car for travelling around and got what I needed, some money behind me, enough to move out and rent a flat. It wasn't too far away from my parents and I still had a lot of meals there. It was a basement flat, but it was furnished and tidy. I had a telephone installed that was quite a luxury, but I needed it. The Black Market was very lucrative indeed, but like most things I did it was a means to an end. My parents had an idea what I was up to but never asked questions.

I needed to meet the "right" type of person next. I was never a drinker really but there was a pub nearby that always seemed to have flashy cars outside. To me, rightly or wrongly, that was an indication of wealth. I started going to this hostelry and would go in at about 6pm when it was already busy with people holding "court" at the bar. It was that type of place and I didn't know anyone. I had had some business cards printed and called myself a consulting engineer. I also added a B.Sc. to the end of my name to give me a bit of gravitas. I was confident in being able to deal with any questions if they arose, but they never did. If I called myself an engineer then I was one.

How did I meet my first "victim" as they called them at the trial? Actually that's an easy question to answer, we found each other, well sort of. A well-dressed man, about my age I thought. I had seen him every time I had been in there and noticed that the wallet he carried in his inside breast pocket always seemed to have a lot of cash in it. He was carrying a pint from the bar and I bumped into him with sufficient force to cause him to spill some of it down his jacket. I was full of apologies and gave him my handkerchief to clean up the mess. I offered to have it cleaned for him but he said it was all right. We exchanged cards though and shook hands.

This was my introduction to Jack Norton. His business card said Property Management.

Chapter 7

JOHN PATRICK NORTON was born in Leeds in 1910. He was known as Jack from an early age. His untimely, and unwarranted, death occurred when he was just 32 years old. He had never married. He was the only child of Reginald and Elizabeth Norton (Reg and Lizzy). He went to a grammar school and left with the usual qualifications at that time, but it didn't matter, he was always going to go into the family business which was Property Management. There was a good sized portfolio of both house rentals and commercial properties. Jack started off in the office, which was actually a room in their house, and learned the ropes. He was a quick learner and bright as a button. He was a very pleasant and affable young man. As the years went by he became more and more involved and would go to house auctions with Reg. There was a technique to buying houses and Jack acquired it. He had contacts, through his local pub, of repossessions of properties that were coming onto the market as well. Business was business and a bargain is always a bargain. It was a simple philosophy but it worked for him.

His parents were no longer young so he started to take some pressure off them. He was the sole collector of the rental incomes from the properties and he had also acquired half a dozen properties of his own. Good, long-term investments. As befitting the image he was trying to build for himself, he drove an MG sports car. It was his pride and joy and cared for like a small child.

When the "Call Up" papers arrived he was at his wit's end. He didn't want to fight and he didn't want to be called a coward, as some conscientious objectors had been called. He had talked about running away to Scotland, nowhere in particular, just Scotland. His parents certainly didn't want him to go, not for altruistic reasons, but purely personal ones. They didn't want their only child to be killed.

Then he met Jenkins whom he and his parents saw as their salvation…

Chapter 8

HE TOLD me all about what he did and we would meet up most evenings. He seemed to like his beer whilst I made mine last. When the conversation came round to me, it was all made up of course, but plausible. After a few weeks he pulled me to one side and said that he wanted to talk to me in private. He had found me out was my first thought but no, it wasn't anything to do with me at all.

I suggested that we went outside and we did. "Can I come straight to the point?" he started with. "Have you managed to avoid being called up or are you classified as being reserved?" alluding to my "profession".

"Reserved occupation although the R.A.F. would have been my choice", I lied. The reality was I had been sent my call up papers but had returned them saying, "Not known at this address".

"The thing is," he continued, "They have been chasing me and I am running out of ideas. " I might be able to help you but it might cost you," I said, as ever I was thinking about a financial benefit to me but not having an idea what I could do for him. Looking back, it was a risky strategy, but ultimately it paid off. I wasn't ready yet to carry out what I had in mind, I didn't have anywhere to do it and more importantly then, could I actually carry it out?

Then, what I would refer to as fate took a hand. I was driving out of Leeds and over the River Aire at Crown Point Bridge when, 200 yards on the left, I saw a sign that said "Outbuilding to let – apply within." And I did exactly that. I had found my factory as I preferred to call it.

It wasn't really a factory, it was a dirty old single storey building. I met the owner, the chap who owned the foundry next door, Douglas Dean, and we arranged that I would have it for £1.10s a week. Through him, and our meeting, I met Veronica of course, she was his daughter. I did a lot of tidying up inside, well I hired some labourers to do it for me. From what I could gather it had been used as some sort of wood store and canteen, but had fallen into disrepair. It was lovely and private, with a lockable solid wooden gate leading from the main road outside. There was only one door, made of wood, into the actual building and I bought a very secure padlock for it. Outside was an area of rough ground, a scruffy, dirty area leading to a six foot high brick wall that used to have an access door in it. It had been bricked up for security, Douglas told me.

I paid for six months' rent in advance and set up Jenkins Engineering. I arranged accounts with local suppliers of 45 gallon oil drums, three of them, and three carboys of sulphuric acid. I always paid my accounts on time. Using forged references I took a chance that they wouldn't be taken up; they never were.

The acid came in glass carboys wrapped in straw with a skull and crossbones label on each of them to indicate that it was a dangerous and corrosive substance. I would later be able to vouch for just how dangerous it was…

I went for dinner at the Nortons' house quite a few times; his mother was a really good cook and they were lovely people. I got to know them rather well, but of course I needed to. I was planning ahead. The last time I was there with Jack, we, I mean me, discussed how he could avoid the authorities until the war was over. I told them I knew some people up in Scotland and would arrange for him to go there. I was in my element; I would sort out a new name and get him *a bank account so that money from his properties could be sent to him. All lies of course. They were very grateful and thought that it was a marvellous idea, and so did I. He would probably have to sell his car (or rather I would) as he might be traced the next time it needed taxing. He would soon be able to get another, even another MG, I ventured. They asked how much this would cost. How would I know that?*

"How about me working for you collecting the rents that Jack collects and sorting out repairs that he does? You pay me a small salary and it takes the strain off you a bit, how's that?"

I had thought of that in a flash. Lizzy looked across to Reg and said, "That sounds like a very good idea indeed, are you sure you have the time to do it Nick with your business interests?"

Chapter 9

THE ARRANGEMENT WAS THIS; I would call for him in the morning and we would drive in convoy. I had mentioned to Jack that I needed to pick up something from my factory on the way but we would only be delayed for a few minutes. I pulled up on the road outside, it was a quiet Sunday morning as I recall, I opened the gates and we drove in. I pointed out where he should park his car. I asked him if he wanted to have a look inside. As he sat in his car I unlocked the padlock on the door and opened it. It was dark inside so I turned the lights on. I motioned for him to come and join me. I had, behind my back, in my right hand, a piece of lead piping that was there when I moved in. I had placed it on the shelf behind the door. When he came through the door, his jaw dropped at the surroundings he was looking at; it was not what he was expecting and neither was what would come next. He turned around to take in even more and I hit him on the back of his head as hard as I could. He dropped to the floor, but had I killed him? I tried to move his body with my foot and could not move him. I knelt down and felt for a pulse in his neck and on his wrist, nothing was evident and then I noticed a pool of blood, getting ever larger, on the floor emanating from his head wound.(It took ages to mop it up afterwards.) I was shaking like a leaf.

Half an hour passed and I had stopped shaking by now and once more felt for a pulse. He seemed to be dead. I didn't feel anything, I thought I would but I didn't. I went through his pockets and removed all his possessions. Some loose change, £25 in cash in his wallet and his keys for the car. In his waistcoat pocket was a gold Albert watch on a chain, I had always wanted one of those but, on turning it over, I saw that it was engraved with the initials J.P.N. I had better not wear it when I next saw his parents! I removed his clothes until he was down to his vest and underpants. It was a pity that none of his clothing would fit as he was a man of taste and always dressed well.

I rolled an oil drum onto to its side, tugged and pulled to get Jack inside then managed to stand it upright. I removed the straw from the outside of one of the acid jars and rolled it too, nearer to where the drum was. I tried to pick it up to pour the contents inside. I could not even move it! How foolish of me, I couldn't grip it and there were no lifting handles on it. I needed a pump or something similar. Thanks to a very helpful man in a hardware store just down the road, I found what I was looking for. It was a stirrup pump. He told me how to use it; I didn't tell him what I was using it for of course! I paid in cash, thanks to the money that Jack had, another irony. I got back, assembled it, put on my long rubber gloves, apron, bought from separate shops, and set to transferring the acid into the oil drum. I used all three of the carboys. I would have to order some more, but not yet.

The fumes began to rise. I stepped outside, leaving the door open, to where the MG was parked and had a rummage inside. A Gladstone bag contained enough information about his own properties that I would need later. It also had the list of properties where rent was collected. Perfect, just perfect. The car was in excellent condition and I would have no trouble selling it. Forging the logbook would be easy, one owner from new, me!

I went back inside and was almost overcome by the fumes. I coughed, spluttered and nearly passed out. I ran outside for some fresh air.

It must be the acid reacting with the body, how long would it all take? I locked up and left his car where it was. At my flat, I made a new logbook with a fictitious name, but real address on it. I was quite pleased with it. I decided to leave well alone with the body in the drum for a couple of days. The chances of anyone discovering it were virtually nil. I went to the "factory" the next day but only to pick up the MG that I then drove to Manchester and sold.

I told the salesman at the dealership that I was emigrating but he could not have cared where I was going. He got a bargain and I got £80 in cash. I caught a train back to Leeds and picked my own car back up. I was tempted to have a look inside but resisted the temptation.

Two days had elapsed so I called on Reg and Lizzy Norton and told them that Jack had been safely delivered to his final destination and in a way that wasn't a lie.

I told them I would be visiting him from time to time but he would not be able to telephone them. I spun them a yarn about phones being monitored etc. They believed me, but why wouldn't they?

The next day it was time to have a look at how things were progressing. I opened the door and in I went, no fumes, thank goodness, although there was an awful smell. I looked inside the oil drum and it was just sludge, a dark brown sludge, just as the mouse had looked in Lincoln Prison. I gave it a stir with a long piece of scrap wood and it just felt like a gooey liquid. To test my theory I had to empty the oil drum. I certainly couldn't move it, it was far too heavy. I would have to use a bucket; there was one, an old one, so I used that to empty the contents away. I poured the remains of Jack away outside on the open ground, bucket by bucket until the bucket would not reach in anymore. I rolled the drum outside and tipped it over. I was tempted to say a prayer but resisted the temptation; it was too late for prayers. The rain and seepage through the earth would do the rest. I was exhausted. Had I done it? Had I committed a crime that would never be detected?

Yes, I thought I had.

I had learned lessons from this, the most important being some form of protection from the fumes. I would address this the next time; I was not in a hurry.

I spent the next few weeks establishing myself as a rent collector for the Nortons. In the spare time I had, I was working on the documents I would need for disposing of the properties that Jack had owned. Powers of Attorney, Title Deeds and the like. I knew what was needed. I would eventually instruct a solicitor to deal with the conveyancing and transferring of the monies.

I travelled to Scotland where I sent a postcard from Jack and arranged, through contacts in the "Black Market", to send them at regular intervals to his parents, no questions asked, of course. I was pleased with the handwriting and his Reg and Lizzy had no reason to suspect a thing. They were happy, their son was alive and well and the business was in safe hands, i.e. mine. As far as they were concerned I was sending a cheque every month to Jack except, of course, I wasn't; there was no cheque and my bank balance grew every month. I saw them fairly regularly and had more of Lizzie's delightful cooking.

As Jack's properties were separate from the family business, his parents never found out. I sold the houses as individual units to private purchasers. I didn't want word getting back through the grapevine to his parents, and it never did.

In all of this, the matters that brought me to where I am now, I wasn't greedy although it may have looked as if I was. I just thought I deserved what they had. That's why I chose them.

Now, I thought, it was time to move up in the world after all; thanks to the money from the sale of Jack's properties, I could afford to.

Chapter 10

THE ISOLA BELLA HOTEL in Harrogate first opened its doors as a hotel in 1908.

In Edwardian times it had been a very large family home, but running costs were high and it had been put onto the market. The purchasers, an Italian family from northern Italy, had connections in the area and had seen the potential of it. After they had completed the purchase of the property, the hotel, as it would now be known, was sympathetically extended in Yorkshire stone to match the rest of the building.

The family name was da Luca, and the current owners were the son and his English wife, Paulo and Geraldine. In this partnership, Paulo was behind the scenes, mainly in the kitchen, with Geraldine being very much front of house. They had met in London whilst training in catering and hospitality. A wedding had followed in the fullness of time and Geraldine became part of the family business. They had two children, two girls. They were good hoteliers and a lovely family.

Harrogate had long been established as a spa town and

people travelled from all over the country to "take the waters". It was a genteel and refined town, both to visit and to live. These factors, and others, led to the large number of elderly people wishing to spend the rest of their days there. They had decided to enter this market rather than the normal type of hotel with its comings and goings. It was a wise choice. The Isola Bella had built up a well-deserved reputation for providing good food and safe and secure accommodation for its guests, or residents, as they were known. The demand outstripped the supply.

Access to medical and dental services was available too that was, of course, then chargeable. The hotel used the services of a local undertaker as and when required, a Mr Benson whose discretion was invaluable.

Residents in the care of the hotel always used the front door; when they were in the care of Mr Benson, the rear door was used. The management didn't want to upset the sensibilities of the residents.

When Jenkins arrived there were thirty five others. They were a mixture of couples, widows and widowers. The majority of them fell into the latter two categories with seventy-five per cent of them being ladies.

Without exception, they were all of independent means. Charges were from £3.15 shillings per person, per week, depending on the size of bedroom. The rooms, whether single or double, were very spacious.

It had a residents' lounge and a dining room that overlooked the gardens. The only extra charges were for laundry and for any alcoholic drinks consumed with meals. Most of the guests kept a bottle of sherry or Scotch whisky in their rooms. It was their choice, although with it being a residential hotel there were no restrictions as such.

War and post war austerity affected the hotel but life at

the hotel carried on. It just became another talking point to be discussed over breakfast, lunch or even dinner.

It was a busy hotel and of course open all year round, as it had to be with its full-time guests. Holidays for the da Lucas were a luxury; they occasionally had a break but nothing more than two or three days at a time.

To them, the business was important; if they got it wrong, the residents might go somewhere else. It could be quite fickle. Although it was not a nursing home and didn't advertise as such, sometimes it felt like one. Indeed, there was a waiting list.

However, in a few short years, two worlds would collide at this hotel. One who would never harm a fly and the other whose stock in trade was killing people.

Chapter 11

I DID LIKE HARROGATE, it suited me, and it suited my aspirations. I now had some money behind me. I had realised over £2,500 from the sales, enough to fund my stay at this hotel for the foreseeable future and buy a car, an Alvis Roadster that I bought for cash. It looked good on the car park of the hotel. It was usually the only other one, apart from the owner's car.

Everyone knew that it was mine.

If I am being candid, I have to say that at the back of mind I had thought that I might find someone who would fit my criteria here.

I dismissed this at once as if anyone "vanished" I would be the number one suspect. There was no getting away from the fact that I had a criminal record.

I moved in and felt completely at home. I had my record collection and I bought a wireless. It was a pity that the hotel didn't have a piano. Mrs da Luca looked a bit starchy and her regular outfit of black suit and white blouse didn't help. After a while I called her by her first name, Geraldine, but she always deferred to me as Mr Jenkins. She seemed to be very efficient but she seemed to pander to the needs of the more elderly ladies.

As I now had a good address, I needed a more professional business card:

Mr Nicholas Jenkins BSc.
Consulting Engineer,
Isola Bella Hotel
9, Southway, Harrogate
Telephone: Harrogate 2705

I HAD them printed and embossed. I had taken a bit of a chance really by including the telephone number of the hotel. It implied that it was my own number but I was selective as to whom I gave the cards, but it looked better and finished off the cards, in my opinion. Most of my correspondence was by letter in any case.

I kept on seeing the Nortons, I had long since decided they were going to be next, with no other living relatives to raise any suspicions. Twelve properties to dispose of once they were out of the way.

I had to keep up the pretence that I was still sending money to Jack in Scotland from his rental properties. Reg even paid for the petrol that I got on the black market. He was a generous man, but after all, as far as he and his wife were concerned, I had saved his son from the chance of being killed in the war. He kept paying me and I kept collecting his rent money.

At the risk of repeating myself, Lizzy was a very good cook. Her Yorkshire puddings were delightful. I stayed for hours on an evening and I was getting to know them rather well. I even stayed overnight from time to time, sleeping in Jack's bedroom. She accepted whatever food and drink I brought without question. Of course she knew how I had obtained it, everyone did. And the postcards kept on being delivered.

Chapter 12

THE NORTONS WERE native to Leeds. Reg was born in 1875 with Lizzy some four years later.

By coincidence, they were both the youngest in their respective families, who had, by now, all passed away. They were educated at local schools and left at the age of fourteen. Reg became an apprentice bricklayer and when Lizzy left school, she went into service in a large house in north Leeds. She graduated to the kitchens and in time became a cook for the family.

Unusually for the time, they married at quite an old age in comparison to their contemporaries. Reg being thirty-five years old and Lizzy, thirty-one. Jack came along in 1910 and was indulged, although not spoilt. He was taught to be independent, a trait he retained. After a grammar school education he left his school at the age of fifteen and went into the, by now, well- established family business.

Reg had begun investing in "bricks and mortar" and had invested well. Lizzy had left "service" sometime earlier and became a housewife/book keeper for the business. They had a portfolio of twelve houses which produced a steady, if unspectacular, income.

Reg still kept his hand in with repairs apart from electrical work; he would have been the first to say that he didn't understand it. He was a good and fair landlord, with a very good reputation.

They lived in a three bedroomed, red brick, detached in Roundhay, Leeds, gardens to the front and rear. And a ten minute walk from Roundhay Park with its two lakes.

They had few holidays but a couple of years before the War they had met a "charming couple", a Dr and Mrs Learoyd, whilst on holiday in Torquay. The doctor was a GP in London where they lived near to Kew Gardens. The Nortons and the Learoyds met up every few months for either drinks or a meal, or sometimes both. They enjoyed their trips to London and when the Learoyds travelled to Yorkshire they would invariably travel out to Harrogate and beyond, sometimes to the Yorkshire Dales.

In a story full of irony, this was one of the biggest of them all. Mr and Mrs Norton, victims 2 and 3 and the Learoyds, victims 4 and 5, never met Jenkins together. He was not aware of their friendship until later, much later.

Everyone in their circle of friends knew that when Reg handed over the business to Jack they would take a long cruise to South Africa. It was a long-held ambition. They had even talked about living there.

They enjoyed the regular visits by Nick Jenkins; he was, in the absence of their only child, almost like a surrogate son. He was good company, an ideal luncheon guest and was, in their view, honest.

Jenkins continued the good work for the Nortons. Some of the tenants, if they saw Mr Norton out and about, said what a charming man Nick was. It pleased Reg, it pleased him no end.

He did like Nick being part of the "family" and, of course, how could he and his wife forget that he had helped Jack to "disappear," although not in the way that they thought.

Chapter 13

Miss Kathleen Hackett was a sixty-year-old spinster when she moved into the Isola Bella Hotel in the spring on 1927.

She had been privately educated and when her formal education concluded, she stayed at home looking after her, by now, elderly parents. She was the youngest child of six siblings, all of whom married and left home. Her father was a mill owner in the Halifax area and was on the brink of retirement. By the standards of the day, they were quite well off.

From an early age Kathleen, never any abbreviated form, always Kathleen, wanted to teach. Her parents had other ideas for her but died within a short space of time of each other. She obtained a position as a governess as a stepping-stone to teaching. She invested her share of the estate from the will of her parents.

She left the family she had been with after two years with impeccable references and this, without doubt, helped her to attain a place in a preparatory school on the outskirts of Harrogate. It was for girls between the ages of five and ten years. It was a private school and she lived in. She lived quite frugally.

She taught English, both grammar and literature, and took to it well. She was loved by the children and admired by staff and parents alike. In time, she rose to be the headmistress, retiring in 1927. Although she never married, she had "walked out" with many a young man when she was younger. Her career always came first though. The children were her life.

Her pension was more than adequate and she received an annuity from the estate of her long since departed parents. She didn't want to live alone in a house; she wanted some company, like-minded people to either socialise with or not. She was a good Bridge player too, a cerebral and social pastime, she thought. This particular hotel fitted the bill for her.

In the summer of 1939, two months before the outbreak of war, Miss Hackett was introduced to a new resident.

At the time, Kathleen had been there the longest and it was as such that she met this latest addition to the residents, Mrs Amelia Sanders. They smiled, shook hands politely and the friendship, which was to span ten years, started there and then.

Even at her advanced age, Kathleen Hackett was sprightly, intelligent and very articulate and was proud of these facets of her makeup. She had seen people come and go but such was the way of life and death in a residential hotel.

These two ladies took their meals together, breakfast, lunch and dinner at 8.30am, 12.30pm and 6.30pm respectively. They were never short of conversation topics.

Much, much later they would occasionally share a table with a Mr Jenkins. Miss Hackett thought him a bit too loud for her taste but Mrs Sanders seemed to be beguiled by some of his stories. Which of course they were.

Once a week she and Mrs Sanders, weather permitting, would go for afternoon tea to Betty's of Harrogate, a very fashionable establishment. They usually chose a Tuesday, they always chose 3.30pm. The same table, overlooking Valley Gardens where the views changed with the seasons. Their conversation very rarely did, they would pass comment, or rather Mrs Sanders did, on the clothes that the other people were wearing, what they had overheard them talking about and the like. Mrs Sanders was a bit of a gossip really. Miss Hackett was not and invariably kept her own council. It really was a case of opposites attract.

Once every two weeks the ladies had their hair done at the same salon, Madam Alicia of Harrogate was the rather grand name of this well-known, and well-patronized salon. In the communal waiting area, the occasional tables were replete with all the latest glossy magazines of the day that were replenished on a weekly or monthly basis, according to publication dates. Mrs Sanders had a stylist by the name of Mr Andre, in the salon at any rate; Miss Hackett's went by the salon name of Mr Ivan.

Hair was styled in curtained, individual cubicles and washed by whichever apprentice or junior was free. A permanent wave, colloquially called a perm, could take between three to four hours and the cost was £2.2 shillings (two guineas).

Part way through whichever treatment the clients had chosen, one of the juniors would always remind Mr Andre not to forget the appointment with Mrs Lyons in a few minutes. It took a little while for Mrs Sanders to understand this; Miss. Hackett caught on very quickly.

It was a code to remind the stylist that his cup of tea was ready. (Mrs Lyons being a nom de plume for the Lyons tea that the salon used). It became a regular talking point. The ladies usually had a cut and dry, sitting with their heads immersed in one of the huge hair dryers that all salons used.

Perms were for special occasions such as a Xmas Dinner and Dance at one of the grander Harrogate Hotels.

The walk or stroll back to the hotel usually took about fifteen minutes if the weather was kind. On an evening, after dinner, they would invariably partake in a game of Bridge; they played as partners and never lost a game. It was not played for any financial rewards but it kept the brain active.

Miss Hackett was in the rudest of health but over the years, Mrs Sanders suffered from a variety of ailments, in particular a gallstone problem. There was talk of a future surgical procedure if the problem got worse.

Kathleen was an avid reader, her favourite genre being crime fiction, with her favourite author being Agatha Christie who by now had a link with Harrogate. In 1926, the year before she took up residence, Miss Christie had sparked off a nationwide manhunt when she vanished, seemingly without trace, from her home in the south west of England.

She was missing for eleven days until she was found, safe and well, at the Old Swan Hotel in the town.

How she got there remained a mystery worthy of one of her own novels. The best, the only, official solution was that she suffered from amnesia.

Kathleen had read all of the published books by this

lady. The fact that she had usually solved the murder well before the ending didn't spoil her enjoyment one iota.

She was not to know, of course, that she would be involved in a "who dunnit" of her own, one that she would help to solve…

Chapter 14

I HAD BEEN DELAYING INTRODUCING Jack back into his parent's lives for as long as I could. Not that I physically could, of course. The war was over after all. They kept asking me when he would be able to come back. I kept saying that it might not be safe, as people had been arrested for avoiding conscription, and for helping people avoid it.

Matters reached a head when my finances were in a perilous state.

I liked to gamble, as I have said before, but I had been rash with some large bets going down. My credit with the bookmakers I used was almost in the "red". The bigger the race meeting, the bigger the bets I made, and the more I lost.

I needed more funds.

I routinely went to my "factory" and always looked in on Douglas Dean, just to show my face and have a cup of tea with him. It was a change from seeing him at his house. He was never part of my plans, and he would have been missed too much anyway.

I inspected the now badly oxidised oil drums and put them outside; my goodness that acid was certainly corrosive. I ordered another six of them and six carboys of acid. They were quickly delivered and I was there to help unload them. I had also bought a sack barrow to move the acid inside without hurting myself. It would also come in handy for moving the full drums later. I had also bought a gas mask from an Army surplus store.

I called the Nortons from a telephone box early one morning and told them that Jack was safely back in Leeds. I would collect them in an hour and travel the short distance to see him. In the car, they could not contain their excitement. I opened the main gates and drove in. "Don't worry about what it looks like outside, it's what's inside that matters, the owner hasn't got around to tidying it up yet," I said, having seen the look on Lizzy's face.

The day before I had unlocked the padlock and left the door slightly open in anticipation of what was to follow. The lead piping was on its usual shelf to the right of the entrance. I suggested that "we do this" one at a time. "Come on Lizzy, the wait is nearly over," I said as I helped her out of the car. "Be back in a minute Reg". In response he said, "I wonder if he's changed much."

She turned left; I reached for the piece of piping and instantly hit her on the back of her head, through the scarf she was wearing. Before she fell forward, I instinctively caught her and laid her down against the side of a wall. She didn't weigh very much. I put the lead pipe back where I had retrieved it from and went to collect Reg. It was drizzling outside and Reg was holding an umbrella as he got out of the car unaided. "You won't need that Reg. Just close your eyes and I will lead you in," I said, adding a sense of drama to the occasion. I led him by his jacket sleeve and over the threshold.

His eyes were still closed as I flicked off his hat and delivered a blow to his head in the same way as Lizzy moments earlier. His weight didn't matter, I let him fall to the ground. They both seemed to be dead but, as with their son, I checked pulses. I undressed Reg but for the sake of her dignity, I left Lizzy as she was, apart from taking off her shoes.

I removed the rings from her fingers that I later pawned. Reg had a silver cigarette case, some cash, a lighter and house and car keys. I also took off his shoes.

I rolled two fresh drums onto their sides and bundled Reg and Lizzy inside each one. I lifted them up to the vertical and moved them using the sack barrow to where I wanted them. I moved the acid by the same method; this was much easier than the last time. I put on my protective clothing, the long rubber gloves, the rubber apron and, most important of all, the gas mask.

I let the acid do its work and although it produced fumes, it was not as bad for me thanks to the gas mask. I locked up and went to their house where my presence never aroused any form of suspicion.

I went through all the documents which had been perfectly filed in a cabinet. Each property had its own folder. Purchase price, when it had been bought, rent amounts and when due and the rateable value of each of them. It was wonderful; they would never know how grateful I was. I then set to work with my favourite legal document, Power of Attorney.

I thought that I had better let the neighbours know, out of courtesy of course, that their friends had decided to go to South Africa on an extended holiday. Of the ones that I spoke to, none was in the slightest bit surprised. They had talked about it for years after all. I never found out what the neighbours ever thought had happened to Jack. Maybe they told them that he was missing in action.

I took the documents back to the hotel and worked on them, only breaking for meals. There was a lot to do. I went back to see what progress had been made at the factory. I donned my mask, gloves and apron. I gave the contents a good stir and all seemed well. Four days seemed to be about right for there to be nothing left. Outside it was raining heavily, a Godsend for me. I bucketed, with a new bucket, the remains onto the rough ground as I had done with their son. A family grave I thought! Mother Nature would do the rest. I took the drums back inside and cleaned up a bit. There was some sludge in the bottom of each drum but I left it where it was.

Reg had written, or typed to be accurate, letters to each of his tenants advising them that he was intending to sell their houses. His signature was on them. Except that it wasn't his; that was me, pretending again. I hand delivered them on rent night. Friday night was rent night. They were used to seeing me but the letters were a shock. They had all been long standing tenants, but in my view they weren't paying enough anyway. He had been far too soft with them in my view. Reg preferred keeping them and keeping them happy.

There were quite a few landlords and property companies in Leeds and "we" all knew each other. It would be easier for me, and create less fuss, if I could sell all the houses as a job lot to one of them. But I would need another type of letter, this one would tell anyone that was interested that they had been on holiday to Cape Town and decided to put down roots, in other words to emigrate. It would have to be good and by the time I had finished it, it was. It took me a while, but it was worth the effort. It was all good practise after all.

The properties sold for the going rate, well, slightly less actually; the new owners eventually putting up the rents. The tenants mumbled and grumbled but paid up. Then, whilst on the subject of properties and houses, a complete surprise. The house that the Nortons lived in, the jewel in the crown for me, was rented! They never owned it. Apparently they had never got around to it and never appeared to have much of a rent increase over the years.

Nevertheless, thanks to my "writing skills" and through my efforts I had raised £5,500.

I informed the actual owners of their house about the plans the Nortons had made and they were grateful that I had let them know. I apologised on their behalf for the short notice. I arranged for the house to be emptied and told the neighbours it was going into storage. It actually went, most of it, to the rubbish tip after I had gone through it. I knew a man who emptied it for a few pounds and no questions asked.

I would always return to the hotel on an evening. It was a safe haven for me, somewhere to relax and tell my tales to anyone who would listen.

Chapter 15

I THOUGHT *that if I was ever caught, thanks to Corpus Delicti I could never be charged with murder; nevertheless it did occur to me that I could well be charged with something like unlawful burial or some such offence. I needed an excuse, a medical escape, just in case.*

Veronica was working in the psychiatric unit of a local hospital after a year at a secretarial college and was doing well. She was a clever young woman, so it was no surprise to me. I started quizzing her from time to time about the symptoms of some of the patients she wrote reports on. No names, that would have been unethical. She thought that I was just interested in what she did; I was, but not in the way she thought. I was particularly interested in schizophrenia.

I spent many a long hour discussing many different types of mental illness with Veronica. I had ruled a lot out but also ruled some in until I decided that it would be schizophrenia if I ever needed it.

I never planned to get caught, that goes without saying.

I know that Veronica will not read any of this but I am so pleased that she came into my life, but I used her, just as much as I used anyone else.

My reasoning was that if I was ever charged with anything I would pretend to be mad. After all, would a sane person do what I had done? Schizophrenia would get me sectioned under the Mental Health Act. I would be miraculously cured then released.

I have to say though, sat where I am, that things didn't quite go according to plan.

Chapter 16

PETER EDGAR LEAROYD was born in London in 1900. He was the son of a surgeon and it was almost preordained that he would enter the medical profession. He studied at Imperial College in London and graduated with a good degree. He obtained a position at Guy's Hospital and stayed there for many years.

His wife, Alice Dorothea Learoyd nee Schuster, was actually his second wife and he her first husband. She was born in New York in 1915. Her father owned a shoe factory. His wife had been born in England, near to York. In her late teens, after a family squabble, she came back to England and decided to stay. She obtained a position at a famous London department store. It was felt that her "American" accent would attract customers, and it did. It was where she met Dr Learoyd whilst he was shopping. They were instantly attracted to each other and an affair followed.

He had met, fallen in love with and married a nurse at Guy's. She wanted children and he did not. By mutual consent, a divorce was agreed. He admitted adultery.

He became disillusioned with the hustle and bustle of London and with the partners with whom he shared a practice in West London after he had left Guy's. He was ambitious, and after he had married Alice, so was she for him. He wanted his own practice. Alice was getting used to the idea of being a doctor's wife.

It would have to wait though. Out of patriotic duty, he enlisted just after the outbreak of war and joined the Royal Army Medical Corps. (RAMC) He served with distinction and was demobbed with the rank of Captain in this regiment, serving in Africa and Italy in the main.

A practice became available in the Yorkshire Dales and he discussed the possibility of buying it and moving to the village of Middleham with his wife. He had no real idea of where it was but she knew of it. She instantly saw the attraction and talked him into it as she did with most things. Another advantage was that they could see more of their friends, the Nortons, who lived in Leeds. It was less than an hour's drive away.

The practice had a stone-built, three bedroomed house attached to the surgery. During the week, it had a part-time receptionist. It was very self-sufficient. Geographically it covered a large area with the majority of patients being "house calls". He would be expected to deal with births and deaths and everything in between. Alice was looking forward to the social side of what went with being a country GP's wife.

They settled in well and started having what Alice referred to as "soirees". Small dinner parties for local professionals who lived in the village and commuted to either Harrogate or York by road, there was no railway station.

His local hostelry was The Red Dragon in the village, a good half mile walk from his house. Scotch and soda was his tipple, Alice, when she joined him, which was not often, had more temperate habits, in public at any rate. The walk would usually coincide with when the pub opened in the evening, which was at 5.30pm. He tried not to dispense "free" medical advice in those days prior to the formation of the National Health Service (NHS), but it was unavoidable sometimes, and it gained him friends. He often told tales, some tall, some not, of his time in the war. He was a good raconteur.

It was whilst he was in this public house one Sunday lunchtime that the paths of Jenkins and Dr Learoyd would cross for the first time.

For the doctor, the clock to the end of his life had started ticking; he would not live to see the start of the great social change that the NHS would bring…

Chapter 17

I FIRST MET Dr Learoyd on a run out from Harrogate; I seem to recall it was a weekend. I travelled to the area, which was known for its horse racing fraternity and stables, fairly often. Trying, in vain I have to say, to pick up tips. I called into the Red Dragon for a half of bitter. It must have been early as the only other person in there was a man stood at the far end of the bar. He looked a little bit older than I look; dressed casually, wearing Cavalry twill trousers, brown shoes, a green cardigan, and what looked like a regimental tie. I always dressed up when I was in the country, or anywhere for that matter. Tweed suit on this occasion, on my feet I wore brown brogue shoes.

"Forgive me", I said, "I've been trying to place the tie." "RAMC for my troubles," he retorted quick as a flash. I was familiar with what those initials stood for. I went to shake his hand and he said, "Captain, retired, thank God. Live and work here now, I'm the local doctor." That got my attention and it got better. I asked him if he would like a drink, I guessed the answer and I wasn't wrong. "Scotch and Soda please".

"Single or a double?" I said as I introduced myself and told him my made up profession. He asked for a large one and I obliged,

ordering another half of bitter for myself. It might be a long lunchtime and I wanted to pace myself. It became obvious that he liked a drink. The pub began to fill up bit by bit but we kept on talking. He gave me a potted history of his life, which was very interesting, especially the bits about having no relatives and owning a two bedroomed flat in Chelsea, which he rented out. The more he drank, the more he spoke.

Unexpectedly he asked me if I wanted to come to his house for lunch. I was quite hungry and never turned down an opportunity like this. We walked to where he lived, on the outskirts of the village but within sight of it. I hoped that his medical expertise would not be required this afternoon; he had had a lot to drink. I satisfied myself with three halves, which was about my limit anyway.

We walked up the gravel path and the door of the house opened. His wife, Alice, greeted us and I have to say that I have had warmer greetings.

"Alice, would you allow me to introduce my new friend Nick? He lives in Harrogate and he is an engineer". "Pleased to meet you," she said through pursed lips. "Please come in". "Anything to eat darling, we are starving." She stormed off, she really did storm off, through to where the kitchen was. I could hear the sound of doors and cupboards being closed, very loudly. Maybe this was a mistake. In the corner of the living room was an upright piano. His wife came in carrying a tray of tea and some sandwiches, cheese and pickle, as I recall. "Who is the pianist?" I enquired. "No one, it's just for show, why do you ask?"

"I play; shall I play something for you after we have eaten these delicious looking sandwiches?" I don't think she believed me one bit. "What can you play then?" she asked in what I would describe as a sarcastic tone. I think she was expecting me to say that I played songs from the music halls.

"Classical pieces, Chopin is my favourite." It was one of the very few things that I never lied about. I asked for a duster to clean the lid and the keys and started to play for them. I played and they actually applauded me. I stood up and made a theatrical bow. Peter took the

lead and said, "That was beautifully played, you know, from time to time we have dinner parties here, would you like to "Sing for your Supper?" I knew what the figure of speech meant and I said that I would be honoured. I decided there and then that these two would be the next to visit my "factory".

Chapter 18

A FEW DAYS LATER, a handwritten letter arrived at the hotel for me as I came down for lunch. It was an invitation to dinner with the Learoyds. I sent off the enclosed R.S.V.P. almost at once. I must have impressed them. I remember being quite excited at the prospect. I had never been invited to anything before, ever. I began to look through my collection of sheet music and put some recognisable pieces together in my music case. My vanity got the better of me, not for the first time in my life

There were, including me, nine for dinner. Alice offered dry martinis before dinner. I remember the olive. I pretended to enjoy it. I could never see the point in putting an olive in a drink and still can't. Dinner, when it arrived, was delightful, roast lamb and all the trimmings followed by apple crumble and custard. The joys of living in the country, all this food on the doorstep. Peter sat next to me at dinner and whispered, "She didn't cook it you know." Laughing as he spoke. I had guessed as much. "It was cooked by a lady in the village." That didn't stop the compliments flowing in her direction though. Which she accepted.

Alice cleared the table; it was as if the actual cook did not exist. The table was replenished with coffee and brandy; I took my glass of brandy in the direction of the piano and set it down and I played for about an hour.

I sat down again next to Peter and, in the absence of Alice, he said to me, "Come with me, I have something to show you," in slightly slurred speech. We both got up from the table and walked out of the lounge into the hall that led to the staircase. In a cupboard under the stairs, he rummaged around and produced an ex-Army khaki, webbing bag.

Like a conjurer produces a rabbit from a hat he handed me something that was covered in an oily rag and quite heavy. He unwrapped it to reveal a revolver, a bloody revolver. From my little knowledge of weapons I guessed it was Officer Issue and I was right. "Spoils of war, old boy, spoils of war. It's a .38 Webley, complete with ammo. It never saw action though, I killed more people on the operating table than that pistol did." He must have seen the look of astonishment on my face and he quickly corrected himself. "The operating table stuff wasn't true; the ones that died were beyond my help anyway."

"Put it away. Put it away, does Alice know about this?"

"Oh no, she never goes in there, it's where all the cleaning materials are and we have a cleaner. I told her not to look inside the bag and to the best of my knowledge she never has."

He put the service pistol back in its bag and placed it loosely in the cupboard. I couldn't get it out of my mind, it could be really useful to me. To use a racing analogy, "Make every post a winning post".

Alice came back in from the kitchen just as we returned to our seats, none the wiser. She asked her friends if anyone wanted to go for a walk as it was such a pleasant evening. The other three ladies said they would love to join her, and that left the five men. Peter offered cigars, Cuban black market he said. I smiled at even more irony, and accepted. Brandy was offered again. I declined but the others had generous refills. Peter was getting more and more drunk, not a good example for a doctor to set I thought, but good for my purposes. I needed to be sharp if I was to get away with what I was thinking.

I excused myself for a call of nature. The bathroom was upstairs and I had previously noticed that a window at the bottom of the staircase had been opened, to allow for ventilation I imagined. Perfect, it gave access to the rose bushes growing under the window outside. I didn't actually need the toilet but went upstairs and creeped back down and opened the cupboard.

I grabbed the bag, closed the door and placed it and its contents outside in the roses. I went back upstairs as quietly as I had come down. The toilet flushed and I returned to the lounge. The ladies came back a few minutes later and Alice offered tea for them.

I got up and walked in the direction of the piano putting my music away in its case. As I readied myself to leave, and to this day I don't know how I had missed it, I noticed a group photograph on a table in the hall. It was two couples, on holiday by the look of it. It was the Learoyds and the Nortons! My legs turned to jelly and I felt physically sick. They know each other! Do they know about me? No, they can't do, it's just not possible, it is just a massive coincidence. As the blood returned to my face we said our goodbyes and I was thanked profusely. "We must do this again," Alice said and her husband, still sat, agreed with her. He really was the worse for wear by now. And I was in a state of shock! I still had a job to do and managed to regain my composure somehow.

It was dark outside by now, the pitch dark that only seems to happen in the countryside. I said to them all, "Thank you for inviting me, the food was delicious and I enjoyed your company."

I got a round of applause, which was unexpected. "Don't get up, I can see myself out." I did just that, closing the door behind me and hesitating to make sure there was no one coming out to wave me off. It was quiet and the front garden was slightly illuminated by the light from the open window. I bent down, pushing the canvas bag inside my jacket and walked, very briskly, to my car. I placed the bag and my music in the boot, locking it.

I slept fitfully that night and for quite a few after that.

I kept seeing them from time to time, quizzing Peter about the property in London when he had had a few drinks. No mention was ever made of the missing gun, thank goodness, not that I ever thought that it would.

Even if the topic did surface, I would simply have said that I didn't know what he was talking about. I had hidden it in and amongst the rubbish in my "place of work" in Leeds; there was plenty of that about.

In anticipation of what had to follow, I ordered some more acid and some new oil drums. The old ones had corroded quite badly and were of no further use to me. I just put them outside the door.

I travelled to London once or twice with Veronica again taking in the sights, but in particular the sights at one particular location in SW3. As luck would have it, a flat in the same building was available to purchase. I made a note of the telephone number of the agent. The "For Sale" sign said it had a very long lease, so that answered one of my questions without me having to ask.

In conversation with Peter I had mentioned that I was in the process of developing a prototype of a battery driven child's car. He seemed to like the idea and asked me lots of questions about it. I baffled him with science. I needed an investor or, if it was true, I would! I suggested that he should come and have a look at it, if he had the time. He said that would be a good idea but also said that it might have to wait a week or so as they were planning to have a holiday in Whitby. That just could not be allowed to happen. I didn't have them down as "Whitby" people particularly and the expression on my face must have reflected that thought. "It's James Cook, you know, Captain Cook, I'm a great student of his, that's the attraction." "Oh, how very interesting", I lied. "I'll tell you what, why don't I pick you up before you go and drop you back off again?" "Oh I'm sure it will be fine, don't want to put you to any trouble old boy." He kept referring to me as "old boy" but it was just a figure of speech after all. "We will come over tomorrow if you give us the directions and set off from Leeds instead." "I'll tell you what, why don't we meet up at my hotel, have some coffee and then you can follow me; it will be a lot easier and you won't get lost". "Fine, old boy".

We met as arranged and had coffee in the residents' lounge. Peter looked impressed, his wife was non-committal; she was either not a good conversationalist or she didn't take to me. We travelled back to Leeds. I hadn't thought about their car but that would have to go as well of course.

It was a little Morris, nothing much of value, but it would sell nonetheless. I remember thinking, the first time I went to their house, how their car did not go with the image of a country doctor. He always said a car is a car and as long as it got him around, he was all right with that. I could never see Alice sitting in it, not at all.

Since acquiring the revolver I had made up my mind that I was going to dispose of them with it. I was not skilled in its use at all and in fact, apart from loading it, I had not even picked it up since I came into possession of it. I had never taken any particular pleasure in doing what I did, but I was looking forward to getting rid of Alice. Nasty woman in my opinion.

Chapter 19

WE PULLED up outside and I unlocked the double doors of the outer gate. I motioned them to follow me and showed them where to park. Peter wound his window down, "I must say, it's not what I was expecting, is this it old boy?" I bent down and leaned through the window, "Wait till you get inside, it's where the real work takes place."

A thought occurred to me as I was talking to Peter, if I shot him, she, Alice, would hear it and try to run away. The gates were closed but not locked. I decided against the original plan.

I opened his car door and pointed the way to the door to my glorified factory. "Come on, it'll only take a minute." He followed through the old door and stood there in the dust and gloom. I hit him with the lead pipe and he fell backwards into my waiting arms. I lowered him to the ground. I put my head around the door and shouted across to Alice, who was still sat in the car, looking very bored. "Alice, Peter is having a funny turn." She opened the car door, leaving it open, and ran towards me, I felt a sense of relief.

The only thing she felt was an almighty crack to the back of her head. I just let her fall. I had gone off the idea of using the pistol for a couple of reasons. One, I had never fired one before and the bullet *might not hit its intended target, and two, it would make a hell of a lot of noise. It mattered not, they were both very dead. I replaced the piping from where I had picked it up.*

I emptied his pockets and took off his clothing. £35 in cash, a lovely gold monogrammed cigarette case with a matching lighter. I used both of them until, well, until they were taken off me in Harrogate, at the police station. There was nothing much in her handbag of any use to me. House keys as well that I would use later. At the risk of repeating myself, they were dealt with as the others had been. I did though, for the only time, almost enjoy pouring the acid over her.

I covered their car with an old tarpaulin, locked the outside gates and set off back to the hotel. On the outskirts of Leeds, I stopped at a telephone kiosk and rang the hotel in Whitby to cancel the reservation the Learoyds had made. There was a letter of confirmation in Alice's handbag with the number on the letter heading which saved me finding the number. I told them that there was a family crisis, which, of course, wasn't too far from the truth, was it?

Back at the hotel I took afternoon tea with some of the ladies and began to relax. I indulged myself and went for an afternoon nap; I was quite tired after all my exertions.

When it got dark, I would travel to Middleham, no socialising in the pub this time. It was important that no one saw me. Wait a minute, wait just a minute. I knew that they had arranged a locum to stand in for him at the practice, but when from? If he or even she was staying in the house it would present a huge problem. I used a telephone on the outskirts of the village and rang the number. No answer, that was good, but what if they had gone to the pub or for a walk? I had to get into the house to get the papers for the flat in London and the car. I drove through and parked my car at the rear of what looked like some abandoned stables. It was pitch black outside. I had the keys and a torch.

I wore dark clothing, well as dark as I had, and had bought some black plimsolls and some cheap leather gloves. The house looked in darkness. I fiddled with the keys until I found the right one and went in. I had never broken into a house before, I was very nervous.

All the curtains were open, so the light from my torch would potentially give me away. The house was set back from the road but not totally isolated. I heard the sound of an occasional car drive past as I adjusted my eyes to the darkness. Any light at all would be too risky. Moving forwards, I banged my foot against the leg of an unseen table, the collision caused the "group photograph" that I had almost forgotten about to fall over and I put it into my bag. I remembered where I was in relation to the roll top desk that should, hopefully, contain what I was looking for. I had admired this desk as a piece of Victorian furniture the last time I was there.

The moon came out and shone through the windows. A bit of luck, it was just what I needed. I turned the torch on and its light played on the lock, covered by my hand, to prevent the glare from it. I felt the wooden shutter on the desk, it was locked, of course, but why wouldn't it be?

I sat on the floor and looked at the bunch of keys, a small key with a cylindrical centre was what I was looking for, to match the lock. It was small compared to the others on the key chain, but it was there. I inserted it into the lock and felt it give as I turned it. I rolled the desk top back to reveal what was inside.

Underneath the desk were two banks of drawers forming the base of the desk unit. I tried to open one of them and it too was locked. I took a guess that the key for it might be in one of the drawers, people did that, as an extra level of security I recalled. I ferreted around being careful not to make a mess. After I had opened nearly all of the little drawers, I found it.

There were piles and piles of papers. Now this presented a dilemma to me. Should I take them all and sort through them at the hotel? I decided that that was what I would do. I really didn't want to spend any more time in this house than I had to. I needed something to put them in. The bag I had brought with me was far too small. First stop, the cupboard under the stairs, the cupboard where the pistol had been stored.

It was safe to turn on the torch and it illuminated just what I was looking for, an old attaché case. It was empty; it was also perfect for my needs. I piled all the papers into it, from both sides of this unit, locking up afterwards. I stood where I was, listening for any sounds outside. Nothing at all. I moved towards the front door with the key in my hand. I opened it and stepped outside. Door locked I walked towards the safety of my car, I changed my clothing and set off back to Harrogate.

I parked my car in its spot; the hotel was in almost total darkness apart from a few room lights upstairs. I had never returned so late; it was by now well after 11pm. I pressed the night bell, I had not been given a key for such an eventuality, and was let in by the night porter whom I had not previously met. I thought it best to tell him that I was a resident, and I did. "Good evening sir," followed by "Good night sir," was all he said.

I retired to my room and lay on the bed with a huge sense of relief. I undressed and put the case under the bed. Whatever it contained would wait until the morning...

Chapter 20

THE TRIAL WAS due to last three days, Capital case or not,
and Veronica had been notified that she would be required
to give evidence on behalf of the defence. From what I had
heard there was only one other witness for the defence,
apart from Jenkins himself that is, and that was a
psychiatrist. Knowing that I was familiar with the comings
and goings of courtrooms, she had asked if I would come
up to Leeds to, metaphorically, hold her hand. I wasn't
covering the events, I left that to Fleet Street and they
would all be there. My geographical expertise of
journalism didn't extend beyond the Sussex boundary in
any case.

I travelled up to Leeds and stayed with Veronica and
her mother and father. Because her dad had initially rented
out the building that some of the more sensational
newspapers had called "The Factory of Death", he had
provided a witness statement to the Police.

His evidence would not be tested, it was accepted by
both sides. Douglas Dean was full of guilt and remorse and
it had made him rather ill. He thought that he had been

duped by Jenkins. He was not the first, nor the last, to be so used in these sad and tragic events.

I took her out of the house to a nearby park where we sat eating ice creams but the silence between us was deafening. Back home her mum was tending the front garden and smiled, without speaking as we went inside. Veronica went upstairs whilst I sat in the front room with her dad who was asleep in his chair.

Outside, I heard the sound of a bicycle bell ringing. Her mother had moved to the back garden and could not hear the knock on the door. I did and answered it; it was a telegram boy with a telegram for Miss V. Dean. I thanked him and gave him a shilling for his trouble. Veronica came down the stairs, half expecting this message. She took it from me and opened it. The trial was starting tomorrow and she would be required first thing on the second day. I remember telling her not to worry, she would be in and out in a flash and then it would all be over, except of course, it would never be over. Even with Jenkins gone it would never be truly over for her.

We drove into Leeds in plenty of time and I parked as close to the Town Hall, where the trial was taking place, as I could. We walked in through a side entrance and approached Court No. 1. I grabbed hold of a court usher and told him who she was. He asked her to sit on a wooden bench whilst I went downstairs to the cafeteria to get tea for both of us. I gave her the tea, which she drank. Ten or fifteen minutes later the doors the court opened and both public and press filed in and the doors closed with a "No Admittance" sign hanging over the doors, put in place by an usher. I stood up, walked towards him and showed him my press badge. "Sorry sir, it's full to the brim." That was that then, she was on her own, without my moral support.

"Call Veronica Dean," bellowed through the precincts of the court, in spite of the fact she was sat where she was, outside the court itself! I kissed her, as cousins do, on the cheek and in she went. Thirty minutes later the door opened and out she came. Tears were streaming down her face and my handkerchief was offered, and accepted, to mop them up.

As we walked down the steps in the direction of my car, reporters and photographers surrounded us. I took off my jacket and half put it over her head to prevent any useable photographs being taken. Flash bulbs popped, vast amounts of money were offered in exchange for an "exclusive".

Veronica was the prize they were all after but the prize remained unclaimed.

She had given her evidence, when she had told the court, "What a nice man Jenkins was," how he had treated her and what a "gentleman" he was, in her opinion. Evidentially it was worthless, it didn't even paper over the cracks, the cracks that had become chasms.

That June day in 1949 was the last time I saw her until 1966. As we reached the car she said to me, "I don't ever want to talk about that so please don't ask me." For almost twenty years I had kept my word, until that manuscript, that damned manuscript had arrived on my doorstep.

Chapter 21

THE CALL I had thought long and hard about making would have to be via the GPO operator. To a degree, it was almost implied by the tone of the letter that had accompanied the "Thoughts and Ramblings of Jenkins" that I should make contact with her, and so I picked up the telephone.

"Hello, operator, can I help you?"

"Amble 8340, please."

"Just a moment whilst I connect you," said the operator.

The dial tone sounded like a monosyllabic cat, purring and purring but without being answered at the other end. I put the phone down, having thanked the operator who was trying to connect me to my cousin 300 miles away, to the north of Newcastle upon Tyne.

At 9.30 the next morning, a Saturday, I tried again and had more success this time.

"Hello, Amble 8340." It was a man's voice in the lovely, in my opinion, lilt of a North Eastern accent.

"Could I speak to Veronica please?" I said.

"Who shall I say is calling?" replied the, as yet, unknown voice to me.

"Her cousin Max."

"Hold on please," the telephone was put down on a hard surface that amplified in my left ear.

"Max, good to hear your voice, I've been hoping you would contact me; it's been a while hasn't it? How are you?"

She sounded the same as when I we had last spoken.

"I'm very well thank you, not surprisingly I have been reading what you sent me and to get straight to the point I wondered if we could meet up? I can come up and stay in a hotel; I don't want to put you out."

"Nonsense, you can stay with us. It's only a small house but we have a spare single room and I can introduce you to my husband Eddie, he is a lovely man, you'll like him. You know where we are then?" she laughed as she asked the question.

"I've got a map, but I must admit that it was a place I had not come across before."

We arranged a mutual date, I would have to take some time off work and so would she.

Although I had a car, a Triumph Spitfire, which was my pride and joy, I decided that it would be easier to travel by train. Less chance of getting lost too if I was honest.

I travelled up to London and caught the underground to Kings Cross. Seven hours and seven stations later arrived on the banks of the River Tyne, this was a first, even in the war I had never travelled this far. I bought a ticket to Alnwick, which was where Veronica would be meeting me, and rang her to let her know what time it would be. I got off the train in Newcastle upon Tyne and the train continued to Edinburgh. I walked to a smaller platform and waited for my connection. Bang on time, at

6.30pm, the train pulled into this pretty market town, the ancestral home of the Percy family.

A porter approached me and asked if I wanted help with my luggage. I pointed to my solitary case and replied in the negative. It was a nice thought though.

There was a cobbled ramp leading to what passed for a main road. It was quiet, not a sign of anyone, but at least it was dry. An oldish looking, dark coloured, Ford Anglia turned left and onto the cobbles. A solitary female driver lifted a hand from the steering wheel and waved in my direction.

She drove the car to the top of the gently sloping ramp, turned around, and came to where I was stood. She turned off the ignition, opened her door and got out.

We, in a very British way, shook hands politely. "Sorry to hear about your mum and dad," I opened with. It brought back memories of the last time I had seen her when smiles were not on the agenda. The boot was opened and she put my small leather case inside it, it nestled on top of the spare wheel. "You must be hungry." "I am very hungry, the food on the train didn't tempt me at all." I sat in the passenger seat and closed the door after me. My little "sports car" had bucket seats, this Ford Anglia did not, but she told me it was only a short journey to where they lived. It would have been impolite to mention it, so I didn't.

We set off along dark, quiet and bendy roads and chatted all the way, or rather she did. She knew the road well and was a good driver.

We never mentioned the name, the name that she, no doubt, wished she had never heard of and wanted to forget. I of course couldn't get enough of it.

She had lived in this part of the world for the last fifteen years or so having emigrated to Australia as soon as she could. She had stayed with distant relatives on her mother's side that I had no knowledge of. She decided that it wasn't for her and became dreadfully homesick. Like thousands of others, Veronica became known as a "Ten Pound Pom". Part of an assisted passage scheme to populate Australia that cost ten pounds with the proviso you had to stay a minimum of two years. If, like her, you came back for whatever reason, you had to pay your own fare. £120 was the going rate back then, a lot of money that she did not have. Her dad paid for it. After a six-week sea journey, he was there to meet her at Tilbury docks on the Thames.

Through an employment agency in England she had opted for a new beginning in the North East of the country. It had childhood memories of times past when they, as a family, came for holidays to the picturesque village of Warkworth.

Far enough away from Leeds, I thought, but yet close enough for family to visit. The job was in a solicitor's practice in Alnwick as a trainee legal secretary. The salary was good and it had prospects for advancement. She was made to feel welcome and kept herself busy learning the "ropes". Her shorthand and typing skills were invaluable to both her and the practice.

I couldn't help noticing yet another irony, both of them working in a solicitor's office.

She rented a room in a small house in Amble and caught the bus to work each day. The room was like a bed and breakfast with dinner thrown in. There were only two rooms let; a nurse occupied the other. Due to her shift work, their paths hardly ever crossed. Veronica happily stayed here, under Mrs Booth's roof, for two years.

Through a social event organised in Alnwick, she met a

local man, a widower, who was ten years older than she was.

Eddie Loseby was his name and he worked in one of the many coalmines in the area as an under manager. He had started off as a technical apprentice and had spent a lot of time at the coalface. It was hard and dangerous work. In this part of the world, it was either the "pits", as the mines were called, or a life at sea on a trawler. Mining seemed to be slightly less hazardous, but there wasn't much in it. Amble was a thriving fishing port but Eddie was no sailor.

They went out with each other for a while, got engaged and married without fuss, at Newcastle Register Office. Her parents witnessed it, Eddie's parents were both dead and in fact had lived in the house that the "new" Mr and Mrs Loseby now occupied.

As interesting as our journey had been, and it had been, it was now over. She skimmed over some of her life, safe to say that they didn't have children.

I never asked why, nor did I ever ask about her husband's first wife.

Chapter 22

THE CAR PULLED up outside a row of through terraced houses and, with a hint of synchronicity, the front door to the house opened at the same time the car doors opened. Standing in the doorway was a very well-built man who wouldn't have looked out of place in the front row of a rugby scrum.

I held my case in my left hand and proffered my right hand to his right hand. He introduced himself and asked if I wanted a cup of tea. I nodded and said that I did. We went inside with Veronica behind me closing the door.

The house was smaller than I had imagined. I was shown in to what was called the "front room". In the south of the country, we would call it a reception room, but no matter. There was a table set for dinner with four chairs and a checked tablecloth. A salt and pepper glass cruet set were in the centre with bottles of red and brown sauce flanking them. The "back room" was a kitchen which led out to a walled garden and then to a narrow back street. The whole house was spick and span, well decorated and furnished. In one corner of the room was the, by now, ubiquitous television set standing on four wooden legs.

I was guided up the stairs to the room I would be sleeping in, put my case on the single bed and came back downstairs. I was greeted by a huge casserole dish placed on a cork mat. "Tea" was ready, not dinner, it was tea, it was the North East. Veronica lifted the glass lid of this Pyrex dish to reveal a layer of suet dumplings on top of what looked like meat and vegetables. I have always loved stew and dumplings, my mouth was watering, it was really. Veronica said, "Hope you like it." Like it? I was in food heaven. Washed down with Newcastle Brown Ale, that was a first. I had seconds; it was a delicious meal.

Earlier this year England had won the World Cup and the whole country was still talking about it. Eddie said that he had been to Roker Park in Sunderland to see Italy play Chile. They had bought the television set to watch the final. He was a massive Newcastle fan and with me following Brighton, we had a lot in common.

I offered to wash up and Eddie dried. It was good to see that "Fairy Liquid" had made its way up the A1! I was offered a cup of cocoa before going to bed but the thought of it took me instantly back to my time in the Army and I politely declined the offer of it. I went upstairs, unpacked my pyjamas and was out like the light I had just switched off.

I had a good night's sleep and I was woken by a knock at the door announcing a cup of tea. I washed, shaved, changed, and came downstairs. The table was set for breakfast like a boarding house. I opted for cornflakes, toast and jam. I dried this time, not as many plates as last night; we stood next to reach other and didn't talk. It seemed to be an uneasy silence with neither of us knowing what might, or might not come next.

I stood, wondering if this had been the right thing to do. Should I have travelled up here to unearth who knows what? The more I thought about it the less sure I was. Nevertheless, she had invited me. She had not read any of the manuscript, she said she never would, I had. Did that give me an advantage?

It was obvious to think, but this would go one of two ways…

Chapter 23

THE RADIO WAS TUNED into the BBC Light Programme and she asked me if I wanted it on or off. I wasn't listening to it anyway. She switched it off.

Before I could say anything else, she started to speak.

"I was fifteen when I first met him at my dad's factory. It was in the summer because I had just finished at school and it was before I went to shorthand and typing college. My dad was going to pay the fees for me."

"What was Jenkins doing there?"

He came to the factory to see about renting the old outbuilding that was to rent. There was a sign outside it."

"What were your first impressions of him?"

"I will never forget it as long as I live, I had an instant schoolgirl crush on him. He was charming you know. The type of person that opens doors and gives up his seat on the bus. Not that he ever travelled by bus. Smartly dressed, he spoke well and I could not take my eyes off him. I was smitten, yes, that's the word, smitten by him. My experience with the opposite sex was limited so I had nothing to compare him with, that's what's so hard"

"What's so hard?"

"The fact, and it is a fact, that he murdered all those people and indirectly I benefited from what he did. It almost destroyed me"

She had started to cry a little and retrieved a handkerchief from the sleeve of her cardigan. I stood up and put the kettle on. I made some more tea and she composed herself.

"I'm fine now, can we just get it over with please?"

"Only if you want to. I don't give a damn about Jenkins; it's you I care about." I was tempted to put my arms around her but she was sat down and anyway I didn't think it would have been appropriate.

"I honestly had no idea where the money came from for the hotels, the food and the cars. As far as I was concerned, he was a successful businessman and he wanted to spoil me. I was flattered and loved the attention."

She continued, more relaxed now I thought after having got the initial burst out in the air, "He took me to Royal Ascot you know."

"Isn't that the place where they wear top hats and the ladies wear their finest dresses?" I had seen newsreels at the cinema; it was way out of my league, even if I liked horseracing, which I did not.

"Oh yes, but he didn't wear a top hat, he gave me some money to buy a new dress. I went to Harrogate and treated myself. I threw it away after all this; I couldn't bear to even look at it, too many bad memories. "

Trying to lighten the mood, if that was possible, I said to her, "Did you have any winners?"

"Not once and neither did he, he tore the tickets up and threw them on the floor after each race. He never got annoyed but I could tell he wasn't happy."

"He wanted the building as some sort of workshop for

his engineering business. I had no idea what he did and didn't care. What an utter fool I was, a stupid, gullible, love struck schoolgirl."

"Didn't the fact he was more than twice your age bother you?"

"Not in the slightest," her smile returned but it was a wry smile.

"It's hard to explain, and believe me I have thought long and hard about it over the years, it never was a physical relationship in the same way I was attracted to Eddie. I still don't know the answer."

"When he and my Dad had finished their meeting he started a conversation with me. He asked what sort of music I liked, my favourite type of food, that sort of thing. Of course, he was trying to impress me. I was fifteen years old for goodness sake, I didn't know anything. Did I have a favourite composer? Did I like French food? I did say that I liked the music of Glen Miller, that was the only composer I knew, that's if he was one. I know he was a bandleader. He had a habit of pausing when he was speaking as if everything he was saying or would say he had thought about. But when you are as good a liar as he was I suppose you would have to think about what you said more than most people, because none of it was true was it?"

She shuffled in her seat and took out a packet of cigarettes from her cardigan pocket. I had no idea that she smoked. She saw me looking at her and said; "It's all right, Eddie knows." I took out my lighter and lit it for her, accepting one.

"He was a good talker, and good company to be with. He seemed very worldly, but there again I only had my dad to compare him with and they were like chalk and cheese.

My dad was far more down to earth, I think pragmatic would be the word to describe him. I loved him and my mum and I miss them both." We finished our cigarettes and sat in silence for a few minutes. How brave was she telling me all this, I knew that we were related but my God, it must have taken some courage. Maybe it was cathartic, better out than in perhaps.

"They talked, Nick and dad, he had asked to be called Nick almost at once. Dad told him what he did at the foundry, making parts for tanks and such like. His employees were working twelve-hour shifts, six days a week. The furnaces had to cool down and have new linings put in each Sunday, if you know anything about how they work." I professed to not knowing anything about how they worked. "I saw them shake hands and just before he left he said to me that he would be seeing a lot more of me. My face must have gone many shades of red with blushing but inwardly I was very happy."

"Do you want some more tea or a coffee", I asked.

"Coffee please, it's in the cupboard over the cooker, milk and one sugar; you know where the fridge is."

I opened the cupboard and took out a screw-topped jar of instant coffee. I made one for both of us. I never took to instant coffee if I am being honest but a couple of digestive biscuits helped it go down. We both dunked them and laughed.

"I did see a lot more of him; he became friends with all of us. Mum loved him or loved the joints of meat he brought round on Sunday lunchtimes. He never seemed to bother about rationing; I never gave it a thought but I know mum and dad asked each other. A dozen eggs from a "farmer friend", bacon and sausages, it was like a food Christmas most Sundays. A couple of bottles of beer too. He was never a big drinker. I was allowed a small glass of beer. He brought classical records with him that we played on our gramophone and listened to after lunch. He would stand and pretend to conduct the orchestra; he was a bit of a show off. He never offered to wash or dry though, maybe he thought he had done his bit by providing the food."

"He first asked me out, or he asked dad if it would be all right. I actually overheard him telling my parents that there would be no "hanky-panky". I knew what that meant, and do you know something Max? There never was, not in all the time I knew him, he treated me like a lady, not a hint or innuendo to do with sex."

Cousin or not, I was feeling distinctly uncomfortable and I am sure that she was. I was grateful for her candour and told her so.

"He took me to concerts, The Halle Orchestra and ballets at Harrogate Royal Hall. He was so knowledgeable and, to me, so worldly. I did enjoy them and he would explain what it was about, which was fairly often to start with."

Chapter 24

"WE GOT some strange looks sometimes; we looked like father and daughter. Was I in love with him? I'm still not sure, maybe I was, I just loved the attention, who wouldn't?"

She had obtained a position in in a local hospital, in the psychiatric wing, as a shorthand typist, courtesy of her new diploma funded by her parents. She caught the tram to and from work. She was asked out a lot by handsome young doctors and even porters, but always said that she was "spoken for". In her mind she was. Jenkins seemed to have increased her maturity.

"From what I heard about during the trial I realised that me working where I did was useful to him. He asked me lots of questions but I thought that he was just interested in what I was doing. The longer I worked there, the more he asked. How could I not have realised? He used me like he used everybody else in his life. As for being mad? He was no madder than you or I. I should be grateful that he didn't kill me as well I suppose."

I did not pursue that line. I did not want to ask why she

thought that. Even with my journalist's hat on, it was a question too far.

Just to reiterate what she had said earlier, "We always stayed in separate rooms in the hotels, he would kiss me on the cheek as we said goodnight to each other."

I got the picture and I believed her.

As if reliving the events she continued, "He took me to all the best shops and stores like Harrods and Selfridges and all the places the tourists go. One of his favourite places, if not his favourite place, was Madame Tussauds Waxworks. We would go straight to the Chamber of Horrors and look at his favourite exhibit, the Brides in the Bath Killer, I think he was called Smith."

She started to laugh, it was nothing that I had said, I hadn't said a word. The laughter, in an instant, turned to tears, floods of tears rolling down her cheek, then it hit me why.

It was because that within 24 hours of Jenkins' execution his wax effigy was on display in that same chamber. People queued along Marylebone Road and paid £1.10 shillings to see the latest addition. It was displayed wearing the actual suit and shirt that he was hanged in. The only additions were a necktie and his shoes had laces in them. It really was a supreme irony, one that was not lost on my cousin…

I got up, put my arms around her and lifted her out of the chair. I walked the few yards into the kitchen, filled up the kettle and put it on one of the gas rings on the cooker. Tea was the solution, a cup of tea. More tea…

It was time for me to put a stop to this. I had heard enough and I didn't want to upset her any more. We drank the tea and smoked in silence. I looked through the window and drizzle or no drizzle I suggested that we should go for a walk.

We walked to the harbour, the bustling little harbour with its twin jetties jutting out into the cold, dark, North Sea. Gulls flew overhead as incoming trawlers disgorged their catches on the quayside. We were quite wet and I felt so sorry for her. We stood looking seawards, "I never went to see him you know, where he was, and he never asked me to although he wrote quite a lot. I never replied, I couldn't bring myself to."

"I know that you didn't mean to upset me, Max, I was just a silly little girl that he turned into a princess. Eddie is very good to me and he is a good man, but do I love him? Do I love him like I thought I loved Nick? I don't know and I never will. I hope that I don't sound ungrateful."

I treated it like the rhetorical question I think it was supposed to be. We walked back. I dried off and left. I would never return, but how much damage had I caused?

On my way to the railway station, a final thought occurred to me, did Eddie know?

Chapter 25

I WOKE UP, put on my dressing gown and went to the bathroom, washed and shaved and walked back to my room. There was no one around, it was still quite early I suppose, about 8 o'clock. I sat in an armchair and had a glance at the Daily Telegraph that had been left outside my door. I would read it over breakfast, I usually did.

I remembered the attaché case then and retrieved it from under the bed. It wasn't safe here at all; the cleaners might find it. I opened it without giving the initials P.E.L. that had been embossed into the leather a second thought. I spread the contents onto the bed and started to look through the documents. Then I changed my mind, I put it all back and into the wardrobe whilst I went down for breakfast.

It was quiet in the dining room, a quick bite to eat then back upstairs to examine my potential "treasure trove". As usual, I was spending what I thought I would make before I had it.

I tipped it all out on the bed and sorted through it. The car logbook was easy to find and would be easy to deal with. I looked and looked and there was nothing at all to do with the Chelsea property. There were some insurance papers, some stuff from the Army, his Army pension was quite generous but I couldn't claim that, although it crossed my mind. Some British Medical Association documents and other ancillary paperwork. I was in a quandary, without the title deeds, I could not sell the flat, if I couldn't sell the flat I was going to be very short of money. I looked repeatedly, nothing. An envelope that I hadn't opened, addressed to Peter in Middleham. It was from a building society about the flat. The bloody thing, excuse my language, was subject to a mortgage; he had told me that he had owned it for years. According to this document, he had purchased it just before he moved to the Dales. It had another twenty three years left on it! This presented a problem, a huge problem. Far too complex to deal with. He had lied to me and probably other people as well about owning it. It was let and the rent would pay for the mortgage with maybe a bit left over. I decided against going down the road of dealing with his bank to get the rent made payable to me, way too dangerous I thought. I was furious, but couldn't show it as the cleaning lady knocked at the door and asked if "I was decent".

The wolves were at the door and I had no solution, or had I? But first things first. Off to Leeds to dispose of the Learoyds and their car. I put the case under my arm and into the boot of my car and drove to Leeds. I opened up the gates and drove in, parking next to where their car was, still under its tarpaulin. I moved it back, as it was where its owners would soon be deposited. I put on some coveralls and did what I had done three times previously. Not a trace, very pleasing. I added some false information to their car logbook and went off to sell it. The best that I was offered was £45 and I had to take it.

That was it then, forty-five measly pounds for all that effort. I threw the case into a corner of the building disturbing the dust as it landed. I put the gun in the case too, I had no use for it and thought that if I sold it on the black market it would lead straight back to me. I left the two empty oil drums outside, next to each other. I thought it was appropriate. His and Hers.

I was now getting desperate for money, so what I had vowed to myself would never happen, had to. I had to look inside the hotel. I had always had someone in mind if it ever came to it.

Mrs Sanders had been here for years. I guessed that she was in her late sixties or early seventies, a handsome woman. She had been a widow for many years. Over the years, I had taken many meals with her and her best friend, Miss Kathleen Hackett. I never quite took to Kathleen and the feeling was mutual, but no matter, she wasn't the one I was interested in. If I needed to, she might come later. Mrs Sanders always seemed to be interested in what I talked about, was it out of politeness or was she genuinely keen about the lies I spun them. I was a great engineer and sometime inventor. I must have been doing well enough, nice car and always well dressed. She seemed to notice if I had bought a new suit and would pass comment on it. Another trip to Gieves and Hawkes, Mr Jenkins?" Alluding to my Savile Row tailors, Mrs Sanders always had something to say.

Chapter 26

Amelia Sanders nee Watkins was born in 1870, making her sixty-nine years of age at the time of her death. She hailed from Ambleside in the English Lake District. Her parents were hoteliers in Windermere. There were older brothers and sisters but they had all died early in life. After a private education, she had started to work in one of the hotels as a management trainee. It was in one of them, she worked in rotation at all three they owned, that she met her future husband.

Norman Sanders was enjoying a weekend break when their paths first crossed. He was born in 1860 and was a Major in the Royal Artillery. Very much a career soldier he had never married and looked like being a bachelor all his life. Amelia was happy being unmarried, she had a few suiters but nothing of a serious nature. They met in 1905 and were mutually attracted. An engagement was announced, with the wedding taking place in 1907. She left the Lakes and lived with her husband in officers' quarters at garrisons and barracks, mainly in York.

She took to the life and when the time came for him to

take his retirement, he was "shooed" into the Diplomatic Service as a military attaché. They were posted to Paris and Brussels, but the jewel in the crown, for her, was a posting to Washington D.C. She really enjoyed it and was a good hostess as she needed to be to fill the role of an attaché's wife.

When war broke out in 1914, they stayed in post and remained there for the duration. When America entered the First World War in 1917, they became even busier. The social events subsided, it was not a time for such matters.

Retirement beckoned for the Major so in 1919 they returned to England. They came back to a changed country, almost unrecognisable from when they had left. A move to Bournemouth seemed to be the right thing to do; neither of them had ever been there, but they seemed to think it would fill their requirements. They bought a two bedroomed flat overlooking the English Channel. They enjoyed their time together and were happy in retirement. They never had children. Major Sanders died suddenly though, from an undiagnosed heart condition.

She was devastated and she was alone. Through an advertisement in "The Lady", she was made aware of this lovely sounding hotel in Harrogate; she knew the hotel trade inside and out. A visit was made and it seemed to fit the bill. She was introduced to Miss Hackett and in conversation with her, it seemed to fit all her needs. She moved in in 1939; she was a very wealthy widow a fact that would, many years later and in the hotel she intended to spend the rest of days in, not go unnoticed by another resident.

Chapter 27

I DID ENJOY HER COMPANY; she was an interesting person. She used to tell me about her time in America and the other places she had been. I had never been out of the country, never possessed a passport. By her stories it was obvious to me that she had a fair amount of money behind her, but if I am being honest, it wasn't until I was getting desperate that she entered my thoughts in that way. But enter my thoughts she did and stayed there.

In conversation after dinner she started telling me that she had an idea for making acrylic fingernails. It seemed like a good idea to her. I had never heard of such things but she seemed to have done her homework on the subject. More importantly, she asked if I, as an engineer/inventor, could help her with the manufacture of them. Could I make them in the factory that I had, she asked.

I didn't need to make anything up to get her to where I wanted her to be.

That was the turning point, fate, call it what you will. She was playing into my hands. "I'll tell you what, why don't we have a spot of lunch and then go through to Leeds and have a look at what we can do. I'm not making any promises, but let's see what we can come up with," I said to her.

She was full of enthusiasm and we made an appointment for a few days hence. I needed the time, to buy more acid and check the drums. The acid was duly delivered; I was set up. I did have misgivings though; this could not be any closer to home for me if it went wrong.

I arranged to pick her up outside the entrance to Valley Gardens; I had told her I was doing some business nearby and it was easier for me. I could pick her up from the hotel if she wanted, but hoped that she wouldn't want that, too many nosey and inquisitive people for my liking. She was dressed in her finery, perhaps a tad overdressed for my liking. Far too much fur, maybe she was trying to impress me? I was already there when she arrived. I got out of the car and opened the door to let her in. I suggested that we go to the factory first and she was all right with that. Thirty five minutes later we pulled up outside on the road. I looked around to make sure no one was about apart from passing cars.

The main goods entrance for the foundry was at the back so that was clear. I opened the wooden doors and drove through; it was getting to be automatic now. As on previous occasions, I got out and opened the door itself. Politely, I opened the door to the car and helped her out. I took her arm as the car was quite low down; she was quite well built. I would find out just how well built she was a few minutes later.

As usual, the lead piping, my trusted weapon of choice, was behind the door on the shelf. I led her in and she stood with a look of what I can only describe as astonishment on her face as she took in her surroundings. As she turned around, I hit her and let her fall. I lit up a cigarette, smoked it, and examined her.

She was quite dead. I picked up her fur hat that had bloodstains on it, as did the fur coat itself. No matter, I would get them dry cleaned and pawn them later. Leeds had a lot of these types of places and I had used a lot of them. I started to undress her and put her clothing into a pile. She was wearing a good selection of rings and I took those off her fingers. I emptied the contents of her handbag onto the floor. I had already decided that for the whole plan to work I would have to gather up whatever she had at the hotel and then leave, but in my haste to carry out this killing I have to say that I hadn't really thought it through.

I concentrated on what I had to do. I put a drum on its side and tried to put her into it. My goodness she was heavy, the heaviest that I had done. I seem to recall I strained my back with the exertion. I got her in and struggled to lift the drum up. It got part way up then I had to let go of it. I could hardly get someone to help me. I put the sack barrow at the sealed end and eventually got it upright. I had to rest, I was sweating profusely. I put on my protective clothing and the gas mask and set to work. I finished up and collected the coat, the hat and her jewellery.

The dry cleaners was my first stop. They would be ready in a few days and they gave me a receipt that I put in my outside jacket pocket. The jewellery was pawned and realised £250; it was good quality stuff. For some strange reason I used my own name but with a false address; I wasn't thinking that anyone would be any the wiser though. I couldn't honestly remember whether I had used this pawnbroker before. Maybe I should have been more careful.

I returned to the hotel, rested and then went out again, had a simple meal of poached eggs on toast at a café I frequented. I returned to the hotel much later and went straight to bed; I was quite worn out.

Chapter 28

ON THE MORNING of January the 14th 1949, Miss Kathleen
Hackett came down for breakfast at almost exactly 8.30am.
Under her left arm, she carried a copy of The Times. The
selection of clocks that did chime, they didn't all, rang in
unison on the half hour; she smiled to herself, proud of her
punctuality.

The Christmas decorations had been put away for
another year on twelfth night, as they always were, even
the decorations were regimented. The memories of the
festive season stored away for another year. As she
descended the staircase, she was greeted by the "new girl"
on reception, as Peggy Black had become known.

Peggy was nineteen years of age, a trainee, and lived
close enough to the hotel to be able to cycle to and from
work. Her regular hours of work were from 7.30am until
5pm with a half hour for lunch, five days a week. Once a
month her duties meant that she covered the weekend and
she had days off in lieu. She had worked in the hotel
during her summer holidays from school so she knew the
family. The only problem she had encountered thus far

had been to remember the names of the residents. For some reason she never forgot either Miss Hackett or Mrs Sanders.

"Good morning Miss Hackett", "Good morning Peggy", was not the opening line of a conversation, it was an accepted neutral, polite, greeting. It had no deep meaning.

Unusually for her, Miss Hackett that is, she had not had dinner in the hotel the night before. She had been "pestered" to try a new French restaurant in town by Mrs Blackburn, another long-term resident. She had finally acquiesced. Mrs Sanders had been asked but had declined the invitation. Mrs Blackburn made the reservation a week in advance, just to make sure they had a table. They had enjoyed the food and the change of scenery, but Blanche Blackburn was not a good conversationalist, certainly not in Mrs Sanders' league. They shared a half bottle of red wine and reminisced all evening. If truth be told, Miss Hackett was relieved when the evening drew to a close.

When they returned to the hotel, on foot and in the drizzle, which they had both anticipated and prepared for, umbrellas ready and in use, the lounge was deserted. They bade each other goodnight as they ascended the staircase. "Good night and God bless" was how most, if not all of the ladies said goodnight to each other. It was perhaps an homage to their Victorian upbringings.

After the "conversation" with Peggy, Miss Hackett walked across the freshly Hoovered Axminster carpet and into the dining room that favoured the same patterned carpet. The tables were all set for breakfast.

In a corner of the room, at his usual table, sat Jenkins who was eating some toast and reading the Daily Telegraph. She took her seat to await the arrival of Mrs Sanders as she usually did.

She took her seat and unfolded the linen napkin, which she placed over her knees. Her eyes glanced sideways and noticed that Mr Jenkins had his tucked into the collar of his shirt. A bit uncouth, she had always thought. The breakfast menu, as with the other meals, was on a printed card held in place in brass circular holders. Kathleen thought that they resembled cut off artillery shells. On a morning, these cards were superfluous, as breakfast never varied and, for that matter, neither did lunch or dinner.

Tinned grapefruit, a slice of bacon and an egg with the option of baked beans or tomatoes. Rationing was still in place, but overall the food was of a good standard, the residents expected it. Jenkins always had toast, marmalade and coffee. Even the "younger" guests were creatures of habit.

She was reading her newspaper, whilst waiting for her food, but where was Mrs Sanders? To within a minute or two Miss Hackett and Mrs Sanders were almost synchronised in their arrival, not just for breakfast, but for every meal. She paused from reading, pulled her chair back and stood up, trying to catch the attention of Peggy at the reception desk; she was on the telephone but waved an acknowledgement.

The call finished, "Have you seen Mrs Sanders this morning?"

"No I haven't seen her yet Miss Hackett," Peggy said whilst still on the telephone.

Jenkins was reading his newspaper but was aware of the conversation that had just taken place. The dining area was not a particularly large room.

"Everything all right Miss H?" This mode of address was quite irritating to her but it seemed to be the way that he referred to everyone. It was always, Mr T, Mrs W or

Miss H in her case, it was annoying. On reflection it was just one of his idiosyncrasies that she wasn't keen on.

Both the ladies had had many a long conversation about this and him in general. Although Jenkins wasn't from London, by using this form of address he sounded like she imagined a "Spiv" would sound. A Black marketeer perhaps? Not that she had ever met one, or had she without realising?

"No fine thank you Mr Jenkins." It was never Nick although he had offered that form of address. Wherever Mrs Sanders was it was no concern of his, she thought. A freshly made pot of tea arrived but still Mrs Sanders had not. Miss Hackett's food arrived but she was too concerned to start eating. In her world, this was almost incomprehensible; Amelia was always punctual.

She went to the desk and asked Peggy to fetch the manager. She wanted answers, maybe Mrs da Luca could provide them, and surely she would know where she was, she knew everything when it came to the residents. Maybe she had been rushed into hospital? A moment or two later, Geraldine da Luca arrived and was appraised of Kathleen's concerns. She took stock of the situation but in all her many years as an hotelier this was a first. If Mrs Sanders had died in her sleep in her room, the problem would be resolved; she had dealt with this aspect many times, and it did go with the territory after all.

On her mental checklist the room was the first port of call. She went behind the reception desk and noticed at once that two keys were hanging from the relevant hook; there should have been just the one. If Mrs Sanders was in residence she would have the other. The keys were of the generic variety with a brass disc as an identifier that simply had "Hotel Isola Bella" engraved on one side and "If found please hand me in", on the other.

Politeness and decorum dictated that that a knock on the door should be made rather than go straight in.

"Mrs Sanders are you in there? Is everything all right with you?" asked Mrs da Luca.

Silence… broken only by cleaning taking place further along the corridor. The key was inserted into the door lock, the handle was turned and the door opened inwards.

"Mrs Sanders? Are you in?"

The bed had not been slept in. On a bedside table lay an Agatha Christie, loaned by Miss Hackett, its last read page being marked with a leather bookmark, a souvenir or memento of Eastbourne.

The two ladies, divided by more than a generation, looked at each other without speaking. Their concern was tangible. They were worried and now said so. The wardrobes were opened to see if anything was missing. Two items, only one stood out, the mink coat and its matching hat. It was Amelia's favourite winter coat. Even in her extensive range of clothing, it stood out.

A cursory search of the dressing table revealed that her "daytime" jewellery was missing. A wedding ring, a diamond solitaire engagement ring that she always wore on the traditional "third finger left hand", an Australian opal that she wore on the opposite hand, bought by her husband, was her favourite piece.

The room was closed and locked behind them. Geraldine caught the eye of the housekeeper who was wheeling the latest model vacuum cleaner towards them and asked her not to touch this room. She agreed without asking why. Leave it as it was for when she came back, it wouldn't be right to search any more.

This duo, the owner and the guest, came down the staircase and as they reached the halfway point they noticed Jenkins stood at the desk in the process of handing his key to Peggy.

He walked out of the hotel without looking back. He took out the cars keys from his right hand trouser pocket. One for the lock and the other for the ignition. He sat in the driver's seat, adjusted the rear view mirror that never needed adjusting, it was just a habit as was saying, "first time every time" to himself, alluding to the fact that the car, an Alvis, started the first time he turned the ignition on. The car was a drop head coupe and had cost some £1400 including purchase tax. A detached house could have been purchased for the same money. In his mind though, not as many people would see it.

The car looked out of place on the car park; it was the only vehicle as none of the other residents had need of one. The de Luca family car was parked at the rear of the hotel. He set off to go to Leeds, he needed to check the progress of what he had started.

When he arrived, it was not good news; as he stirred the gooey liquid in the oil drum he came across solid body parts. He should have added more acid and he had run out of it. It would be all gone in a day or so, no need to worry.

Chapter 29

ALTHOUGH MRS SANDERS was in general good health, her GP, Dr Mitchell, had advised her to stop smoking and to lose some weight. She chose to ignore what he had said. She did though have an ongoing gallstone problem.

As a precaution, and as part of the process of elimination, Peggy was asked by Mrs da Luca to contact the Harrogate District Hospital. For good measure she also contacted the two main hospitals in Leeds. No one by that name or description had been treated or admitted. This was now becoming serious, not yet sinister, but very concerning nonetheless.

Mrs da Luca walked into the dining room, cleared her throat and made an announcement to all present.

"I am really sorry to disturb you but could I have your attention please?" The sound of cutlery being put down could be heard and newspapers being refolded. She continued, "Just out of interest, has anyone any idea where Mrs Sanders might be? We can't seem to locate her."

It sounded like a line from a farce, the type of comedic play regularly performed in post war theatres up and down the land. She had no need to worry about her delivery though; it was said with such gravitas and sincerity that all the assembled guests listened to every word. They were fond of Geraldine and although they were, after all, a regular source of income for her and her family, the feeling was reciprocated.

One of the guests, sat by herself, Mrs Enid Long, said in a timid voice.

"Wasn't yesterday the day she was going over to Leeds with Mr Jenkins to see his factory? I'm sure I overheard them discussing this, I don't normally listen to other people's conversations."

She was very embarrassed at this disclosure but wanted to help. As she finished, Kathleen Hackett was aware of her own face changing from its normal pallor to what she imagined as cardinal red. Inwardly she thought, you stupid, foolish woman, of course that's what she was going to do. It had completely slipped her mind, how could it have? She knew all about it, of course she did, she had even said to Amelia. "You must be out of your mind to even think about such a thing," alluding to the plastic finger nails.

"Oh please Kathleen, let me indulge myself, it's harmless and it might even work. Nick has every confidence that it will work."

"You know best Amelia," Kathleen Hackett had said somewhat dismissively.

They always knew what the other was doing; even if it wasn't being done together.

In a state of utter embarrassment Kathleen said to Geraldine, "Might I have a word in private please?"

Sensing something was not right she led Kathleen into the hotel office at the rear.

"I feel such a fool, a silly old fool. She told me several

days ago that she was having what she said was a business meeting with Mr Jenkins and he was taking her to Leeds to discuss this silly finger nail thing, in my opinion. She said that she and Mr Jenkins had talked a lot about it but he would have to take her to his factory to see whether he could do it or not. My thoughts were that he would know whether he could do it or not without taking her there. She did like the attention he gave her, quite the charmer but not my cup of tea. She had more money than sense sometimes; it's not as if she needed the money. In my view, she was trying to invent something that didn't need inventing."

Chapter 30

Geraldine summoned a member of her staff to bring some tea. Tea normally helped with most problems but it wouldn't help this one. On her mental checklist there was only one more thing to do and that was to contact the Police. This would not be delegated to a member of staff; this would be done by her and her alone…

"Harrogate Police Station, PC Binns speaking."

Geraldine, away from prying ears and eyes, had hung the "Do Not Disturb" sign on the outside door handle of her office. She had kept her husband up to date with developments so far, of which there were few. She explained the situation as she saw it.

There was a pause and the officer started to ask her a series of questions. He didn't appear to have any sense of urgency and in her view, this matter needed both urgency and action.

"How long has she been missing?"

"Has she done this before?"

"What was she wearing"?

It was as if he was reading from a script and ticking off boxes…

"She hasn't run away to get married has she?"

This was the last straw, was he making a joke of this? He didn't sound funny, why had he said that?

Not knowing the age of the officer Geraldine then said:

"Young man, this is not a matter for levity at all."

She continued,

"Put me through to CID please." She was trying her best to remain calm but it was a struggle. She normally had a very even disposition.

"It's not a matter for the CID madam," Binns said.

"Two things," pausing to remember the police officer's name, "PC Binns: one, I'm not a madam and two, I am a personal friend of Detective Sergeant Nolan so please put me through to him."

"Let me see what I can do," he added, with, in her opinion, a very couldn't care less attitude. The call was transferred and in the CID office one of the telephones rang. "Sarge it's for you."

"CID, Sergeant Nolan speaking."

Detective Sergeant Martin Nolan had been a police officer for fifteen years and at his current rank for the past four years. He was married with two children and lived in Pannal, a small village in the direction of Leeds just off the A58. The house was in a small enclave owned by the local authority then let to the Police. (It made transferring from area to area easier if the officers were posted elsewhere).

"Thank the lord for that," she said. The sergeant thought the voice sounded familiar and he replied, "Geraldine, is that you?"

"Yes, it's me."

He was half expecting an invitation for dinner or tea; they had been friends for years and he often popped in for a cup of tea if he was in the area and free. As neither invitation materialised Nolan took the initiative.

"What's the matter?"

"Have you got time to come and see me at the hotel? One of our residents, who has been with us for years, has gone missing and we have no idea where she is.

"We are all very worried that something may have happened to her. I have contacted the hospital and she's not there. It's completely out of character."

"Give me ten minutes."

He took his overcoat from the hat stand near the door and asked his staff who had the keys for the car. He told them where he was going and what it was about. One of the younger detectives said to him, "Have a cup for me Sarge."

The remark was taken in the spirit it had been intended, Nolan smiled and set off.

Five minutes later, he pulled up in the empty car park at the front of the hotel. As he got out of the car, Geraldine was waiting for him at the door. She led him into the lounge and asked him if he wanted tea or coffee.

"Can we have a look in her room first please?"

"Yes, by all means," she replied changing hats from friend to hotel owner, an owner with a missing guest.

Geraldine had her pass key with her as they ascended the stairway to the first floor. Nolan had never been upstairs before, never had the need to. His left hand held the oak bannister, to his right, paintings and old photographs depicting old Italian scenes adorned the walls. Landscapes and old family groups, none of which showed anyone smiling, he observed.

The room door was opened and in they both went, leaving the door ajar. He had left his overcoat and trilby hat in the care of Peggy downstairs and now he took off his suit jacket. He looked all over the room for any signs that might indicate where she might be, even under the bed. Drawers were searched, wardrobes emptied, but there was nothing to indicate what had happened, if anything had that is, or where she might be. He got up from all fours and sat on the bed,

"Tell me all you can about this Jenkins character."

They retired to the lounge where Peggy, without being asked or prompted, had made some coffee and provided a plate of Rich Tea biscuits. Mrs da Luca smiled at her and nodded in appreciation. She then went to her office and retrieved all the information they had about Jenkins. She sat down with Martin as they drank the coffee and ate their biscuits. Cigarettes followed, supplied by the sergeant. The hotel did not have too much information about Mr Jenkins, no next of kin, C of E for religion, single. She noticed, for the first time, a business card in the name of Jenkins in the folder.

"What a bloody cheek, please excuse me for saying that, he has put our telephone number on his card."

"I've heard worse," Nolan said with a smile.

"He pays with a mixture of cash or cheque," and on that topic she said at once, "he is always late settling his account.

"What stood out at once was how young he was in comparison to the other residents. He was a good thirty or forty years younger than most of them."

"Do you happen to know his date of birth and if he has a middle name at all please?" he asked.

She stood up and went back to her office returning a few minutes later.

"Sorry, I had that; I should have brought it with me the first time. His date of birth is 15.02.1908 and I can't see a middle name anywhere, he might have one but he hasn't told us what it is, is it important?"

"Don't worry about it, it's just so that I can run a check on him."

He tried to precis what he had in his head as more coffee arrived. We have a businessman, an engineer or inventor or a bit of both, a snazzy dresser, nice car and always full of himself. No crime in that is there? Always polite and respectful and very well spoken. That was it really, Miss Hackett had always said there was "something about him she didn't like but couldn't put her finger on."

That was neither proof nor evidence.

"What type of car is it that he has?"

"My husband tells me that it is an Alvis roadster or something similar, I don't know anything about cars, I don't drive. He was always taking the ladies out for a spin; like I say, he is a proper show off but they love it, they always come back in one piece," she said, trying to lighten the conversation.

Martin stood up and asked to use the telephone. They walked through to the office. He telephoned the police station and was put through to his office where DC Sutcliffe, the detective with the sense of humour, answered the call.

"Right then young Sutcliffe, pen or pencil and paper in any order you like, time to do some joined up writing."

This was the sergeant's attempt at humour.

"Ready Sarge," came the instant response and he made a note of what Nolan had just gleaned from Mrs da Luca. He replaced the receiver and picked it up again. This call was to the Criminal Record Office (CRO) in Wakefield, the one after that would be back to the hotel to tell his supervisor that nothing was known about this Jenkins person. That's what he thought… the sergeant was on a bit of a wild goose chase, but he kept that particular thought to himself.

"Young" Sutcliffe, Freddy, was actually thirty years of age but the nickname had been with him the whole of his service, which was the last ten years. He did look young. He had been a detective constable for just over three years.

In the office they worked in there were two sergeants and ten constables, a detective inspector, currently on leave, and a detective chief inspector supervised them. It was a busy office.

He dialled the number and spoke to one of the officers in the CRO just over the "border" in the West Riding of Yorkshire. He supplied the information, sat down and lit a cigarette. This will be a quick "nothing known", he had convinced himself.

"Still there?"

"Yes I'm here, anything known?"

Another request for paper to write on, but this time from the records officer.

"Ready when you are."

"Right then, Nicholas Jenkins date of birth February 15th 1908, three convictions recorded."

DC Sutcliffe wrote down the supplied information with a brief account of what the offences involved and sentences had been. He thought to himself, alluding to Martin Nolan, "That's why he's a sergeant."

Straight away, he telephoned the hotel.

What Sutcliffe told him whetted his appetite to meet this Jenkins even more. He hadn't been expecting it that's for sure. Never assume was the mantra he tried to instil in his officers and here he was, assuming there would be nothing known about Mr Nicholas Jenkins. Practise what you preach sprang to mind.

"OK Geraldine, this Jenkins sounds like a con man and

a forger to boot. I can't tell you too much, much as I'd like to. I can't do any more here for time being, so I'll go back to the station. How much does he owe you right now?"

"I think it's about £125 but that includes laundry and drinks."

"That's a lot of money, why so much?"

"It's three months in total. I have been asking him but he keeps fobbing me off. He actually gave me a cheque that was "referred to drawer". He's been like this a lot. I am actually thinking of asking him to leave. Enough is enough."

Nolan's ears pricked up," Have you got his bank account details then?"

"I have the cheque," she said.

None of this felt at all right, but it was barely circumstantial, it was at best conjecture and speculation.

"Would Miss Hackett happen to know where this factory was I wonder?"

They returned to the residents' lounge where Kathleen Hackett was still sat and asked her the question.

"I believe the premises are called the Leeds Foundry. I remember him telling Amelia, Mrs Sanders," she quickly formalised the name of her friend.

"I'm sure she said it was on Black Bull Street just over a river or a canal; it's not an area that I know."

He thanked her for her help; she was still embarrassed and asked to be excused.

"One more thing please, before I go, can we have a look in his room? And before you ask or think about it, I don't need a warrant, it's your hotel and I have your permission don't I?"

"Of course you do."

He needed to know if Jenkins had flown the nest or was he coming back.

Geraldine and Martin walked up again, this time to the second floor. The room looked clean and tidy with no signs of a hurried or sudden departure. A look in the wardrobe seemed to confirm this. At least a dozen suits hung up, all with Savile Row names. Handmade shoes by Church's, maybe the shirts were handmade too. French cologne and gold cufflinks. A gramophone was on a table in a corner, a selection of classical music records at the side. Leather suitcases were under the bed. This was a sartorial goldmine and Nolan had no doubt, no doubt at all, that Jenkins would be returning. It was just a matter of when. The door was closed and locked behind them as they had done with Mrs Sanders' room. The sergeant asked that his office be informed, and himself in particular, as soon as Jenkins returned, no matter what the time of day was.

He walked out to his car and looked up at the hotel. Where was she? Just as importantly, where was he?

Chapter 31

HE DROVE BACK to the Station, thinking on how best to chastise PC Binns for the condescending way he had spoken to Geraldine. He drove through the cast iron Victorian gates to the station and went inside. He bumped into PC Binns who was, in his view, a uniform carrier. The telling off would wait, this inquiry would not. He went to his office and told his staff what they were potentially dealing with. Next step, up the stairs to see his boss.

He walked along the corridor of the two storey building, stopped and knocked at the door with the sign "Detective Chief Inspector Burns" on a polished brass plaque.

Mr Burns, never Richard, his given name, even off duty, was sat at his desk with his in tray deeper than the out tray at the opposite side of his desk. He had his briar pipe, unlit, in the corner of his mouth. His double breasted suit jacket was draped over the back of his chair. He was a very thorough detective and never left anything to chance. He had been in the Police Force for almost twenty-nine years and was looking forward to retiring in the very near future.

Since the Second World War, he had investigated five murders and detected all of them. Without minimising these offences, they were all of a domestic nature. Harrogate was not known for violent crime and he wanted to leave it like that as part of his legacy. Under his command was a team of well-trained detectives. They provided CID cover for not just the town, but the surrounding area as well. It was a large geographical area and covered rural areas too. In rotation, the constables worked the night shift, between 10pm and 6am. The supervisors would be on call, also in rotation, if anything broke that needed their attention and expertise.

"Sit down Martin, what's on your mind?"

"Have you got a few minutes Boss? Well, actually more than a few minutes."

"For you, always." He smiled as he said this. Martin had always got on with Burns and found him very approachable.

"Shall we have some tea?"

"Yes please."

Tea and the Police, Police and tea. A good fit.

Nolan took his time, explaining and outlining exactly what he had been pointed towards via Mrs da Luca and his investigations to date. The DCI methodically filled his pipe from its leather pouch and lit it. At the conclusion, Burns said to his Sergeant,

"What do you think Martin, what's your gut feeling? What's going through your mind as well?"

"Quite honestly Boss, I don't know what to think. I've gone over it and over again and I'm no further forward. Fact: she is missing and she shouldn't be, women like that don't vanish off the face of the earth do they?

"In addition, men like him don't usually stay in hotels, he's a convicted thief and con artist. But is it a case of two and two making five or just four? I hope I am not being too judgemental about him, but it doesn't make sense. Plastic nails for God's sake, sounds like another con to me. Supposed to be a bit of a charmer, charms the birds off the trees. I'll tell you something Sir; he won't bloody well charm me."

"I've listened to what you have told me Martin and I agree with you completely, but at the moment it's purely hypothetical. There could be a rational explanation as to where she is. We don't know her and we don't know him, but you are right it doesn't sound right. We've acted on less in the past haven't we? Who do we know in Leeds?"

"I know one or two very well, through CID courses; it depends on who covers this area."

Richard Burns picked up the telephone and asked the switchboard to connect him to Leeds City Police Headquarters. He was directed to Dewsbury Road Police Station in Leeds. He asked for his opposite number, a Detective Chief Inspector.

"DI Burton, can I help you?"

"Sorry sir he's on leave, will I do?"

"It all depends on whether you cover Black Bull Street?"

Chapter 32

LIKE MOST THINGS in the life of Nicholas Jenkins, the description of his so-called place of work was an exaggeration. His styling of it as a "factory" was grandiose to say the least. A "factory" it was not and never had been. It had, in the past, been used as a works canteen but had fallen into disrepair over the years. Douglas Dean, the owner of it, and the foundry, thought that someone could make use of it, so with that in mind had erected an advertising hoarding at the side of the road. The rent would be £1.10 shillings per week plus rates and utilities. The gas supply had been turned off for safety, but it had electricity and running water.

In reality, it was 1920s brick-built, with a corrugated asbestos roof, a single storey annex to an old established steel foundry in the Hunslet area of Leeds, a heavily industrialised part of the city. It was a ten-minute walk over Crown Point Bridge, one of the bridges that span the River Aire, from the city centre.

It was "L" shaped with the top of the "L" measuring some 15 feet square; overall, it was approximately 60 feet in length. There was an old desk, some metal chairs, a Belfast sink and a gas fired water geyser that no longer worked. In the past someone had erected some wooden shelving. It had become an area for storing rubbish; it was both dusty and grimy. Four unshaded light bulbs hung from the ceiling joists. At the front, allowing access inside, was a quite substantial wooden door secured by a padlock which Jenkins would change for one of his own.

Jenkins had spun his usual web of lies to Mr Dean; he was going to totally transform the place, it would be unrecognisable he had told him. He was right about that. He paid six months' rent in advance and shook hands on the deal. Mr Dean was happy to have a reputable businessman as a tenant.

Jenkins had returned to finish off what he had started with Mrs Sanders, he had never had to rush one before, and he usually had lots of time. This time though he did not have that luxury. Whilst disposing of the remains of Mrs Amelia Sanders he thought to himself, had this been a mistake? Had he chosen the wrong victim? He should not have let his debts mount up in the way that he had.

HE POURED her away onto the ground to join the other five. She was hard work. Next time, and there would have to be a next time, he would be more careful, especially with the size of the person. He was aching all over as he left the drum in situ. The fur coat he had left at the dry cleaners would not be ready for a couple of days, but in the meantime he would pawn the jewellery; that would realise some money.

This building could not have been more perfect for Jenkins. It was about 50 feet away from the perimeter wall of the foundry and had once had an entrance, long since bricked up, leading to the main building. The brick wall extended around the perimeter which gave vehicular access from Black Bull Street itself via a wooden, lockable gate.

The land around, which Jenkins had used as a human dumping ground, resembled a scrap yard in its infancy. Overgrown weeds, bits of wood and metal strewn around on a soil and rubble covering. Two more 45-gallon decaying oil drums stood as sentinels to the door of this annex.

It was to this location on a drizzly and dismal day in January 1949, that Detective Inspector Burton and Detective Constable Les Stead, after being briefed by DCI Burns and DS Nolan from Harrogate CID, went.

Chapter 33

THE DECISION TO walk to this part of their area, their "patch," was taken out of their hands. There was no car; it was being serviced. The drizzle turned to rain and in spite of their headwear and raincoats, neither truly designed to keep out the weather, by the time they got to the premises they were quite wet.

Detective Inspector Charles Edward Burton and Detective Constable Leslie Stead were very experienced detectives. They had worked on a lot of inquiries together, Eddie and Les, where circumstances allowed. They both lived in Leeds; it was a condition of service that the officers in this city force lived within its geographical boundaries. Leeds City Police Force had an establishment of about 1000 officers and was surrounded by Bradford City Force, The West Riding and North Yorkshire Constabularies. Eddie lived with his wife and two children in Headingley in a three bedroomed semi-detached house not too far from the world famous cricket ground that bore the same name. Les lived in Holbeck in a three bedroomed terraced house. He also had two children. In a sporting context, Les wasn't too far away from Elland Road, where Leeds United played football.

It took them fifteen minutes to walk and as they walked they talked about what, if anything, was going to confront them. "Wild Goose Chase" sprang to both of their minds as it had to DC Sutcliffe in Harrogate.

The perimeter gate was locked and surrounded by a tall brick wall.

Question: Wall or gate.

Answer: Neither.

It would look very suspicious and they didn't want the Police being called to investigate the Police. They thought of their own safety because they had no idea what was on the other side of this wall. They could not hear a dog but you never knew (dogs, the natural enemies of both postmen and police officers).

They walked the short distance in the direction of the city centre to what looked like an office entrance. Over the doorway was a keystone with the year 1875 carved in the stone. The letters D&C were entwined to form the name of the company, Dean and Company. There was a small, sliding, glass hatch on the right of the vestibule. A middle-aged lady sat at a telephone switchboard and was answering a call. Behind her, on a desk, was a typewriter. DI Burton knocked on the glass to get the attention of the receptionist although she had seen them. She motioned that she would only be a minute whilst she dealt with what she was doing.

Both men took off their hats and undid the buttons on their very wet raincoats. Raincoats, what a misnomer, they were certainly not rainproof. Perhaps it meant they attracted rain!

The glass slid open, she was used to dealing with commercial travellers plying and trying to sell their wares, but instinct told her these two gentlemen were not in the trade.

Her instincts were correct as Eddie Burton took out his red fabric-backed warrant card and introduced them both.

"You need to speak to Mr Dean, Douglas Dean, he is the owner."

She tried his office but there was no answer so she used the Tannoy system that had recently been installed to call him to the nearest telephone. It was a loudspeaker system set up throughout the foundry to inform staff that they were required or needed on the telephone. The telephone on her desk rang.

"Mr Dean", she said, "will be here in a minute or two."

Douglas Dean came into the reception area via a door. He introduced himself to the officers and they shook hands.

He was aged about forty-five and dressed in a full length brown, smock-type coat that covered, and no doubt afforded some protection to, the three-piece suit he wore under it. They went through the door to the privacy of his office.

Private it may have been but to ears unused to any sort of engineering business, it was noisy. Mr Dean was told what the officers wanted to know and they stressed that this conversation was to go no further, especially if it all came to nothing. The officers did not use the "Wild Goose" figure of speech, they were far too professional.

He was taken aback, no he was horrified, that Nick, Mr Jenkins, could be involved in any sort of crime or a missing widow, or both. He had been to their house lots of times after all. This was preposterous; it must be some sort of bad joke. Was it an anonymous tip off from a business rival he wondered?

The officers were not laughing.

Dean told them exactly how long he had known Jenkins, but more importantly, to him anyway, was the fact that his daughter Veronica had been a very good friend of Jenkins for quite a few years.

"How old is your daughter, Mr Dean?" Les Stead asked.

"She is twenty. He is a complete gentleman and has taught her such a lot about music, opera and ballets."

Stead continued in the same vein,

"How long has she known him for?"

"Since she was fifteen, just after she left school," Dean said.

The policemen resisted, somehow, the temptation to "roll their eyes" but looked at each other nonetheless, without speaking, with raised eyebrows.

"Would you like some tea, officers?" Dean asked.

Tea arrived and was very welcome. He was asked if he had the keys for the outbuilding, as Dean had described it. He had the key for the main gate but not for the door leading into the building they had come to see. It was still raining as they walked back to the gate that Douglas Dean unlocked. It was a larger area than they had been expecting. Mr Dean stopped in his tracks as he walked toward the annex.

"Nothing's changed, it's just as I let it to him years ago. I haven't been in here, didn't need to, it was in safe hands, wasn't it? He paid the rent on time, always in advance."

"What are they for?" he asked, rhetorically, pointing towards the oil drums. Again, in the same rhetorical vein he asked himself. What did he do for a living? Was he really an engineer? This place was a mess, and if the outside was, what would the inside reveal?

DC Stead was asked by his supervisor to see if there was any other way of gaining entry other than by the padlocked door. Dean said there wasn't but Les Stead looked around anyway, peering through the dirty windows.

"We will have to force it then."

In his understandable naivety in these matters Dean added, "Don't you need a warrant for that?"

The Inspector looked at him and said, "Do you own the building Mr Dean."

"Of course I do, I've just told you I do."

"Well then," he paused. "Do we have your permission to take that door off its hinges so that we can get in and see what's inside?"

"Yes, yes, of course you do. I want this matter closing so that we can all get back to work."

"We need some tools then please, a crowbar would be good if you have one," the Inspector continued. Mr Dean returned a few minutes later, he had a three-foot long crowbar but for good measure he had also brought a hammer and a chisel.

Stead had effected this sort of entry before, he was no stranger to a crowbar, usually backed with the warrant they did not need on this occasion. The padlock hasp gave in to a mixture of technique and strength. The wooden door split vertically but the hinges remained intact.

What daylight there was left poured inside this almost derelict building. Burton instinctively felt for a light switch and found one. The lights came on and the dust that had been disturbed formed a halo around the nearest hanging bulb. It was eerie to say the least. Surely, no one works in here do they? Dean was looking even more astonished, if that were possible. He reiterated that Jenkins was an engineer of some sort and inventor even. He even had a business card. He repeated what he had told the officers a short while ago that he not been inside here for years.

This "glorified shed" needed to be searched. The

detectives took off their coats and suit jackets and hung them on the back of a couple of chairs. A bath would beckon at the end of this day that was for sure, they were not looking forward to this. They decided to start at each end, separately, and asked if Mr Dean could possibly bring them tea to drink. On his way to the far end of the annex the Inspector paid close attention to three 45 gallon oil drums, opened at the top. They were not in a good state at all, they seemed to be held together with their welded seams. There was some sort of sludgy residue in the bottom of one of them. At the side of these drums were four empty glass containers, carboys that looked like they had once contained acid.

Schoolboy science reminded him that H2 SO4 was Sulphuric Acid. The slender necks of these vessels were protected by a layer of straw held in place with a wire mesh.

Eddie picked up a long piece of thin wood from the floor and went to the most intact of the drums. He rocked it from side to side but nothing moved. He then broke the skin of this "sludge" to a depth of about three inches, to the bottom of the drum. He withdrew the wood and held it to his nose, which was a huge mistake. At once he started to cough and sneeze simultaneously. To his untrained nose, it smelt like ammonia or the strongest smelling salts he had ever come across. The air around him became "blue" with language the owner of the foundry had not been expecting and neither had Les. Burton threw the piece of wood as far as he could within the confines of the building. It hit a window but did no damage; it had run out of energy. Three drums were outside and a cursory glance indicated there was "sludge" at the bottom of each of them.

Eddie apologised to Mr Dean, who gone outside by now, back out into the rain and fresh air, for his language.

He had had the foresight to bring an umbrella with him though as he returned with the tools.

He asked him if he needed medical attention. The officer answered in the negative, but wasn't too sure, and thanked him for his concern.

Whatever else was or had been in here there was no missing widow. Harrogate needed to be told to allay their fears about Mrs Sanders. In one sense they were relieved, but in another there was still a job to do here. Both officers continued to look around.

In the nearest corner was a huge tarpaulin. Stead lifted it up gingerly; he had been thinking that just in case, it would be safer to treat it as a potential crime scene. It revealed what looked like a coat rack and hanging from it was what looked like a gas mask. But unlike any type of mask he had ever seen.

This mask had what resembled an elephant's trunk dangling at the front. The face part had two glass eyepieces to see through. What was it? The whole country had been issued with gas masks during the war in case of gas attacks that thankfully never materialised, but not masks like this one.

His "discoveries" were only just beginning. Another piece of tarpaulin caught his attention and underneath this was a stirrup pump. A piece of equipment designed to move liquids from one vessel to another. It was DC Stead's turn to use "industrial language" for which he made no apology. These experienced officers did not know what to make of any of this. They surmised that it looked like this acid was being transferred into the oil drums using the pump, but why, for what reason? These questions would not be fully answered for a little while yet.

Their joint attention was now drawn to the desk area on which sat a portable Remington typewriter. Its cover was taken off to reveal a piece of headed notepaper in the carriage. The Isola Bella Hotel was on the top of this sheet of paper.

"Wasn't that the name of the hotel this old dear is missing from?" Les Stead asked his boss.

"The Isola Bella?"

"It most certainly is."

They moved the piece of paper and it looked like a letter was about to be written on it. "Dear Mr," was the only thing on it. There was no date.

Using his initiative, Douglas Dean had been to get two electric torches for them to use. They were gratefully received; the light outside was fading fast and inside was not much better. They shone a light under the metal desk which, in reality, was more like a trestle table. There was a brown leather attaché case with papers sticking out of it. The case was lifted out carefully, by using the zip fastener at the top. They both noticed that it was embossed with the initials P.E.L.

"If his name really is Nicholas Jenkins, who the hell is this P.E.L.?" asked Les.

The case felt heavier than he thought it should and he, Les, decided to empty the contents onto the desk that they had given a bit of a clean with an old rag. Papers fell out, then the distinctive sound of metal on metal made by something wrapped in an old piece of material.

"Bloody hell. It's a gun."

The weapon was lifted by inserting a pencil through the trigger guard. It looked like a .38 Webley service revolver, the type issued to officers in the Army. At its base it had a metal ring where a lanyard would be fed through it. Both men were familiar with firearms; since the end of the war there had been a lot around, many brought home as souvenirs. It was carefully broken open and had six rounds in its revolving chamber. These rounds, the bullets, were emptied into the pocket of Burton's jacket without being touched by their hands. He held the barrel to his nose, now back in working order after his sneezing fit, to try and see if it had been fired recently. It did not appear as if it had. Overall, the weapon was in good condition. Whether this was a crime scene or not it was decided to make it into one. The mood had changed, and not for the better. As they left, a piece of lead piping lay undisturbed and unnoticed, for now, on a shelf behind the door.

There was a protocol to be followed; in the absence of his Detective Chief Inspector the next in the chain of command was Detective Superintendent Alf Barker.

Burton went to the foundry office and asked to use the telephone. Barker was spoken to and asked what Eddie required, initially only a fingerprint officer and photographer, in reality one and the same, was requested.

Barker was a good boss, a very good detective and he was widely respected. He had no plans to visit, as yet.

Whilst Eddie was temporarily absent, Les started looking at the pile of papers now on the desk, wills, letters, mortgage information and conveyancing documents amongst them. None of which bore the name of a Mr Jenkins. He waited for Eddie to return which he did a few minutes later carrying two beakers of hot, steaming tea. It would be the strongest drink they would have for hours. Eddie had told Mr Dean what was happening and told him to return to his business; if anything changed he would be informed. He was advised not to speak to anyone about what was going on.

All Douglas Dean could think about was making sure that his daughter was alive and well. She might be home by now or she might still be at work, she often worked late. He decided to go for the latter option. He hardly ever called her at work. He gave his receptionist the number and the connection was made. Rather than tell her what was happening at the foundry he just made small talk and asked what sort of a day she had had and what her mother might want as a birthday present, in spite of the fact that it wasn't Mrs Dean's birthday for another four months.

"Are you all right dad?" she understandably asked. Her dad reassured her and told her he just felt like a chat, but this was so out of character for him. He told her he would see her later and to come straight home. What should have been a telephone call to ease his mind had had the opposite effect on Veronica. He was greatly relieved that he had spoken to her, lit a cigarette and relaxed as he exhaled the smoke from it.

One final thing that the Leeds detectives had neglected to tell their North Yorkshire counterparts was the lack, the total lack of anything remotely connected with the manufacture of plastic fingernails or anything else connected with engineering or inventing.

The call was made and both sets of officers updated each other. In one sense he had a lot to tell them but in another, he didn't. Until Jenkins returned, DS Nolan would not have much to tell his Leeds colleagues.

Mr Dean, although never having served in any of the armed services, knew what the expression, "line of communication" meant. He asked if his receptionist, Mrs Leak, should stay on. The offer was greatly appreciated and accepted. They continued to search and supervised the fingerprint man who had a long evening in front of him; he knew what he was doing so was left alone.

It was now a waiting game.

Hopefully the call would come through from Harrogate sooner rather than later.

Chapter 34

Mrs da Luca could not contain herself. He's back, he's back, she said to herself. She had been on edge all afternoon. She had tried to reassure her residents that everything would turn out for the best. She walked briskly to her office and dialled the now memorised number of the police station. After being put through, not by the other officer she previously had spoken to thank goodness, she thought, she was informed that DS Nolan was on the other line and would call her back.

"It's Geraldine from the Isola Bella Hotel, let him know that he is back."

"Who is back Mrs da Luca?" asked the unnamed voice.

"Just tell him, he knows all about it."

Martin had finished his call to his counterparts in Leeds and was made aware of the communication.

Jenkins had parked in his spot in the car park. It was a foul day and he was glad to get back. A cup of tea would do the trick, he thought. He walked through the entrance door that had been shut to keep out the rain and into the residents' lounge where he ordered a pot of tea.

He said a few hellos to staff and fellow guests but did not enter into any form of conversation.

He had a lot on his mind and wanted to think.

The tea arrived and, as usual, it was accompanied by a welcome cigarette taken out of his cigarette case. He never smoked in his car.

Nolan shouted across to Sutcliffe, "Jenkins has come back."

The keys for the CID car were in his pocket and ten minutes later they pulled up alongside the only other car in the small car park. A wet but gleaming Alvis. Nolan, it has to be said, looked at the car with a certain amount of envy.

He had dealt with people who had the trappings of luxury before and, generally speaking, they were difficult to deal with. Pains in the backside.

Would Mr Nicholas Jenkins break the mould or would he be the same?

He was about to find out…

Chapter 35

RATHER THAN CAUSE a fuss and to maintain decorum in the hotel, the two police officers stood at the reception desk and looked into the dining room where Jenkins sat, drinking his tea.

The younger and more headstrong officer looked at his Sergeant. If the look had words it would have said, "What are we waiting for?" Jenkins looked across and their eyes met as Nolan walked across to him leaving Sutcliffe behind.

"Good afternoon officer, or is it evening yet?"

"Is it all right if I finish my tea before we talk, that's why you are here isn't it? To talk to me? Shall I order two more cups?" and nodded in the direction of DC Sutcliffe.

In all his service, Nolan had never been more astonished at what Jenkins had just said.

1: That they had been recognised, although maybe that wasn't too surprising really, and

2: The effrontery of the man, inviting them for tea.

Whatever next?

"Yes, we would like to speak to you Mr Jenkins; it is Mr Jenkins isn't it?"

"Oh yes officer, but you seem to have me at a disadvantage, I don't know your names and you know mine."

Nolan did the introductions, formally. The offer of the tea was politely declined. Jenkins finished his tea and stood up. He pushed his chair under the table and as he stood, he fastened the buttons on his single-breasted three-piece suit.

As the duo became a trio Nolan said, "We would like to speak to you regarding the whereabouts of Mrs Amelia Sanders, one of your fellow residents, whom I believe you know."

"Certainly, I will do anything I can to help you, are we going to the police station?"

"I think it would be better than here, don't you?"

They all walked towards the, by now, open front door of the hotel, as the rain had stopped. As they approached the police vehicle, Jenkins paused at his own car and patted the roof of it twice.

"She's mine you know, my only vice."

The officers tried to look suitably unimpressed.

One of the rear doors of the four-door Austin was opened, Jenkins got in with Nolan at his side. Sutcliffe drove the short distance to the station. Through the double swing doors and into a door marked Police only, which was opened with a Yale-type key. The station sergeant greeted them.

"Good afternoon gentleman what can I do for you?"

"Inquiries only, potential witness to a missing person," Nolan said.

"Name and address please?"

Jenkins furnished this officer with that information

which was entered into what was called the "Casual Visitors Book". The old sergeant had seen it all during a very long career that had started after being demobbed from the Army in 1919. Just another witness, another entry in a book that when its pages were full, would be stored away to gather dust he thought.

After he had retired he would "dine out" for years on how he had met Jenkins and, no doubt, helped solve the crimes.

They walked along a narrow corridor towards an interview room. The door was open, a sign that it was not in use. It was sparsely decorated, the walls were a drab green and the linoleum-covered floor was spattered with burns from discarded cigarettes.

An old, dusty, Victorian fireplace, with a gas fire fitted into it, occupied the main wall and above that hung a framed print of the monarch, King George VI. A rectangular table with four chairs completed the inventory, apart from the ubiquitous metal ashtray in the centre of it.

As an "icebreaker" Nolan said, "Well gentlemen, I don't know about you, but I am parched, shall we have some tea?"

Sutcliffe had played this role before and knew exactly what to do. He excused himself and came back a few minutes later carrying a tin tray with three mugs, sugar was in a separate bowl. Jenkins was asked how much sugar he wanted and was served with two teaspoons, as they all were.

This was so very civilised, Jenkins thought, tea, but no biscuits, which was a pity. Almost reflexively; he took out his cigarette case and offered them to the men.

" Not just yet thanks," Nolan said, speaking for the two of them.

"Before you put it away may I have a look at the case, it's rather lovely."

Jenkins was a little flattered by this comment and handed it over. On the front was a cartouche in the shape of a shield inside of which were the initials P.E.L. The man sitting opposite the two detectives had the initials N.J.

P.E.L. rang a bell with the sergeant but not with Sutcliffe who had not been privy to the conversation his sergeant had had with Leeds. Nolan finished his tea, stood up and excused himself. He was away for about ten minutes during which time Jenkins and Sutcliffe made small talk based on the weather, in the main.

Ten productive minutes later Nolan re-entered the interview room. This interview could now start in earnest. To be on the safe side he thought it might be better to administer the Judges' Rules caution. This advises suspects or potential suspects that they do not have to say anything unless they wished to do so. Jenkins nodded in agreement but felt uneasy; why this sudden change in direction? After all, he was only a witness, they had told him that. In the past when he had been in custody, he was already under arrest. Not in this case surely, he thought. He would tell them what they wanted to hear and be back at the hotel in time for dinner.

"When was the last time you saw Mrs Sanders?" began Nolan.

"A couple of days ago I suppose; she was supposed to meet me for a business meeting but she didn't show up."

"A business meeting?"

"That's right, she had some scheme to manufacture false finger nails made from some sort of plastic."

"And your involvement would have been?"

"By profession, I am an engineer and a bit of an inventor so I thought that maybe I could help her. I offered to take her to my factory in Leeds to show her around and discuss if I could make them. I had every confidence that I could."

They knew full well that Jenkins was no more an engineer than they were, but seeing as he had started the deception they carried on with it. Two, or in this case three, can play this game.

"But she didn't turn up? Is that correct?"

"That's, correct. I arranged to see her outside Bettys Tea Rooms. I waited for a good half an hour and then set off to go to Leeds by myself."

The questions, and answers, were being written down verbatim by Sutcliffe in a notebook.

"You are aware, are you not, that she hasn't been seen at your hotel for a number of days now?"

"It's all very strange isn't it? I wish I could help you but I don't know what's happened to her."

"Could I have my cigarette case back?" asked Jenkins.

He was in desperate need of a smoke.

"I'm afraid not Mr Jenkins, I need to keep hold of it for the time being at least."

Trying to gain some sort of control, control that he needed, he then tried a new approach.

"By the way, please call me Nick, everyone does."

Both of the officers assumed wry smiles then Nolan said, "Please have one of my cigarettes; I believe they are the same brand as yours."

Jenkins' mind was racing, but the tobacco helped to relax him. What did Nolan want with the case, what had he found? He had an idea though, of course he did. This detective was not stupid.

Chapter 36

WHAT CAME NEXT WOULD HAVE to be an "Oscar"-winning performance from Jenkins, someone who had never set foot on a stage, never mind a film set.

The detective sergeant took out the case from a brown envelope that now encased it.

"Who is P.E.L.? Mr Jenkins, sorry, Nick? Is it someone that you know or knew?"

"Well actually I did know him, but he died."

"Sorry to hear that," Sutcliffe replied.

Nolan decided to risk everything on a gut feeling: "Did you kill him?"

Jenkins stubbed out his half-smoked cigarette and asked for another one. Matches to light it with were offered, but he was already taking out a gold lighter from his trouser pocket. This lighter, a Dunhill, had the same initials as the case engraved on it. Jenkins, in a very feeble attempt at humour, said, "A matching pair, eh? I suppose you want this as well?"

"And did you?"

"Sorry?"

Nolan wondered what else might be in his pockets, as he had not been under arrest, he had not been searched when he had arrive at the station.

"Stand up and empty your pockets if you don't mind."

He did as requested without question. Loose change, his car and hotel keys in the other pocket. His wallet was inside his jacket pocket. £120 in £5 notes, £3 in £1 notes. A receipt from a dry cleaners and some pawn tickets made up the rest of the contents, save for his driving licence and some business cards. Ignoring these items for the time being Nolan continued in the same vein:

"Did you kill him?"

"Who is P.E.L.? Where can we find him?"

"I'm afraid that you won't be able to find him, ever. He was Dr Peter Learoyd and yes, he is dead."

"Did you kill him? Nolan asked for the third time.

"Look, I like both of you, but let me be frank with you. I killed Mrs Sanders as well as the doctor, his wife and three others quite a few years ago. You will never find a trace of them.

Both the experienced officers reeled at this admission but remained calm, certainly on the outside.

"Why is that, Nick?"

"I dissolved their bodies in sulphuric acid after I killed them. When they had dissolved, I emptied the remains outside my factory in Leeds. They are gone, every last bit of them."

This last statement was said in an almost grandiose manner, something to be proud of.

So that was the connection then, the acid, the oil drums that DI Burton had told them about. God above, this was a horror story, surely they were dealing with a man relieved of his senses, a lunatic. But Jenkins, Nick, had said it in such a matter of fact way, as if talking about a game of cricket or football, without the passion. To say they were incredulous was the understatement of all understatements.

Sutcliffe put his indelible pencil on the table and he and his boss looked at each other, then looked at Jenkins. They were almost lost for words, "shell shocked", they later said.

"For some reason best known to yourself you are playing games with us aren't you? Please tell us that what you have just said is made up."

Jenkins paused for a moment and said in a measured tone:

"Every last word is true."

He picked up the dry cleaning receipt on the table and said, "This is for the fur coat that Mrs Sanders was wearing when I killed her, it got a bit of blood on it. I couldn't sell it like that could I? The pawn ticket is for the jewellery."

This was an intelligent, well-dressed and well-spoken middle-aged man and here he was admitting to killing six people in such a matter of fact way.

The officers tried to absorb this, they never would.

"By the way, you can't charge me with murder, if that's what you are thinking about. I know all about Corpus Delicti, if there is no body there is no crime. No Crime, no trial, it's the law of the land."

Nolan stood up and left the room in search of a uniformed constable to watch Jenkins for a few minutes as he and Sutcliffe had a talk with each other outside of the earshot of this, this potential monster.

"Freddie?" he said to Sutcliffe. "What do you know about Corpus Delicti?"

"Enough to know that what he has just said is utter rubbish," the younger detective said. He continued,

"Anyway, don't you remember that case a few years ago when a man, a cabin steward I think, was convicted of murder when he threw the body of a woman through the porthole of a ship? They never found her body did they, I think was an actress?"

"I remember that now you mention it, made all the headlines in the Sunday papers."

They went back in to see Nick smoking, he had been provided with a cigarette by the young constable, who now left. In the drama that was unfolding, he had just had a walk on part, but one he too would never forget.

"Nick, continued the sergeant, for the first time slightly raising his voice, but not enough to be considered oppressive in any way. "Let me be frank with you as well, who on earth told you that?"

"It's something I have always known, why? Isn't it correct?"

"Whilst neither of us have law degrees we have had a certain amount of training to get where we are, do you accept that?"

"Of course I do."

Taking the lead again, Nolan continued: "In that case let me tell you that Corpus Delicti actually means The Body of Evidence, not, I repeat not, an actual or physical human body. If we, the Police and the Court, can prove that a person existed and then disappeared, for example, but there was enough evidence to suggest this person had been murdered, we can charge people with murder. It's called circumstantial evidence. Can you see that? Did you ever hear of the "Port Hole Murder?"(Alluding to the case that the two officers had discussed outside the room, the case had been given this sobriquet by the Sunday newspapers).

"Should I have heard of it?"

"It was in all the papers a few years ago."

"I don't remember reading it in the Daily Telegraph." The officers watched the colour drain from Jenkins' face in spite of this somewhat glib comment.

"You are now under arrest on suspicion of the murder of Mrs Amelia Sanders, we won't be asking you anything else regarding this."

The room went very quiet,

"Nick, were all the murders you have admitted to committed in Leeds?"

"Yes, all of them, why? Does that make a difference?"

"Yes it makes a huge difference, inasmuch as what we have to do now is lodge you in a cell and let Leeds CID know what you have told us; they will be coming to collect you."

"That's a pity, can't you deal with me?" he asked, more in hope than expectation.

All three stood up and Jenkins began to loosen his necktie, he knew the procedure, knew the ropes. He was flanked by the taller men as they approached the front desk, which was a huge expanse of polished wood.

"Can we book Mr Jenkins in on suspicion of murder please?"

"What murder would that be Sergeant Nolan?" the older sergeant asked in a somewhat sarcastic vein which either was not picked up, or ignored, by Sgt. Nolan.

"The murder of Mrs Amelia Sanders, the lady who went missing from one of our hotels; it happened in Leeds so they will be coming for him as soon as they can."

The paperwork duly done he was led along a white tiled corridor. He had vowed that he would never take this sort of walk again. Tie off, shoes off and the braces that held his trousers up off. He asked for a cup of tea, which would be forthcoming, as would a supply of cigarettes, without matches.

Nolan dashed off to brief DCI Burns upstairs leaving Sutcliffe stood outside the cell. The door would have to be left slightly open during Jenkins' occupancy of it. As it was a potential "Capital Case" he would be on a suicide watch, whether he had shown any suicidal tendencies or not. The same constable they had used the services of before was given this job and was under strict instructions that he was not to talk about what Jenkins had been arrested for, at all.

"Can I ask you a question before you go?" he shouted to Freddie.

He walked back and went into cell, and sat alongside Jenkins on the wooden bed.

"Thank you for looking after me but can you tell me what the chances are of being released from Broadmoor?"

Sutcliffe had vaguely heard of Broadmoor but wasn't sure in what context,

"I don't know, sorry," he said and finished his walk away this time. There were statements to be written by him and Nolan. He found his sergeant and told him what Jenkins had just asked him.

"Make a note of it Freddie, it might be very important."

He then explained what and where Broadmoor was. A hospital for the criminally insane in the south of England. It was where people went if a court judged decided that they could not stand trial due to insanity, or if they were found guilty but insane. There was no time limit on how long the patients stayed there. Some, after many years, had been released.

"Do you think he's mad?"

"No I don't, but for what he is facing it's probably his best shot."

Their DCI came to have a look at Jenkins in the cell but did not speak to him. He was thinking that, due to the lateness of the hour, it might well be better to keep him overnight and for Leeds to collect him in the morning. He asked Martin to speak to them and get their thoughts on this.

In all his service and anyone else's for that matter, Detective Chief Inspector Burns had never heard anything like this. He, following his chain of command, informed the hierarchy at his headquarters.

This was going to be a sensational story when it broke, and break it would he thought as surely as eggs are eggs. But that would be tomorrow. He was proud of his men, so far they had done an excellent job and he told them so. He was secretly very relieved that it was a Leeds job.

Nolan went to the telephone in his now deserted office and rang the foundry. The receptionist went to get DI Burton. Burton, never lost for words, this time was. He agreed that they would be over first thing in the morning and thanked Nolan.

This was now a proper crime scene and would need protecting. After informing the detective superintendent, who was now at home but had furnished Eddie with his home telephone number, he started to try and preserve the area outside the door of the annex. Two uniformed officers were posted at the entrance and would stay in situ until relieved the next morning.

Chapter 37

THE DETECTIVE SUPERINTENDENT HAD, after the call from DI Burton, spoken to the head of the CID in Leeds who in turn had spoken to the Chief Constable. This inquiry looked, and indeed was going to be, unprecedented, not just in Leeds but possibly the whole country. They, Leeds City Police, would be under the microscope. Whatever they did would have to be correct. To that end, a briefing was arranged at the force headquarters for 8am the next morning and a Murder Squad formed through hurriedly arranged contacts and calls throughout the night. For the officers who did not have telephones installed at their houses, uniformed constables paid them a visit.

Alf Barker was the head of this team of seasoned detectives. Many of them, on the face of it, refused to believe that such a thing as had been described to them would, and could, have taken place. Surely this person was making it up. Their collective minds would soon change.

First things first, a team of two detectives and a driver would travel to Harrogate and return with this Jenkins character. Chronologically, the Home Office forensic pathologist would need to be informed as well as the coroner. The pathologist was Dr Ronald Turvey, a very experienced man, he would need to be, this would test even him. DI Burton and DC Stead were selected as interviewing officers, they had started the ball rolling and it was only right that they should see it to its conclusion. Scenes of Crime Officers to assist the pathologist made up the team. There would be no contact with the press and when there was, he, Barker, would arrange a press briefing. He made this point very clearly.

Jenkins was taken from one cell to another and transferred to Dewsbury Road Police Station in Leeds. As at Harrogate, he was watched over with the cell door open pending the arrival of Burton and Stead. They, in the meantime, had returned to Black Bull Street with Alf Barker so he could take in this scene of mass murder, or as much as he could comprehend. This was truly beyond belief, were they actually standing on human remains?

Dr Turvey was the next to arrive and he was fully put in the picture. He needed to know exactly what was supposed to have happened. He was a scientist as well as a doctor of course. It wasn't a large area that he had to investigate, the sheeting had already been removed for his arrival and he walked around the perimeter to start with.

It was then, whilst this investigation at the scene was just getting under way, that the unmistakable sound of flash bulbs popping was heard. Barker rushed out to see press photographers perched on ladders and crates, leaning over the yard wall to get a vantage point.

He was "spitting feathers" and almost beside himself with rage, not just at the photographers, but at whoever had "leaked" this information. Heads would roll, but not yet, there was a job to do here first. He gathered the photographers together at the side of the road and threatened to collectively arrest them all for obstruction if they did not go away.

"Just doing our jobs Mr Barker, come on Alf, can we have a quote," was typical of the retorts made by them. He knew they were just trying to do their jobs, he didn't like it, but that's what they were doing. It did not curb his anger. He summoned a radio car and asked for a uniformed presence outside to keep these "vultures", as he called them, away.

Incongruously, the only thing this achieved was to cause even more attention. He promised them, without any authority at all, a press conference at 4pm the same day at his headquarters.

In view of what Jenkins had told the Harrogate officers, that human beings had been dissolved in sulphuric acid, something the Leeds officers had not been aware of on their first visit, Dr Turvey hoped that he might find something tangible. His luck would be in.

He made up a grid section across the entire affected area by stretching string, held in place with 6-inch nails at each end.

It resembled an archaeological dig and was rudimentary, but it should work. Each square measured approximately 3 feet square and the whole area was about 64 square feet. He could always increase this search area if it was necessary.

He donned wellington boots and set about his grisly business; a scenes of crime officer, similarly attired, was behind him with a selection of brown paper bags of varying sizes.

A photographer completed this small entourage. Only

the pathologist walked on this grid. He prodded and poked each area, disturbing the surface, bending down and breaking up the earth with his gloved hands. His crucial work would take some time, he was fastidious, but he had to be.

Chapter 38

Before they set off to work that morning both Burton and Stead had told their respective wives that it might be a long day and to expect them when they saw them.

The interview room in this Divisional Police Station in Leeds was much the same as in Harrogate, different paintwork, no picture of the monarch though. A table, four chairs and an ashtray, empty for now. An interview room was an interview room. Tea was asked for and ready for them as they brought Jenkins in to be questioned.

Introductions made and Les Stead would be, initially, taking a secondary role in the questioning. He would take the lead from Eddie Burton if an ancillary question needed asking for the sake of clarity or to clear up any potential ambiguities.

Jenkins was reminded that he was still under caution.

"Mr Jenkins," Burton commenced, "Before we start the interview may I just point out one or two things to you, if you don't mind?"

"By all means, but when I was in Harrogate, they called me Nick, you can call me that as well if you want."

The inspector continued, "If you want to address either of us I would prefer it if you would call me Mr Burton and my colleague, DC Stead. If it's all the same to you we will speak to you as Mr Jenkins."

"As you wish officer, sorry, Mr Burton."

"If you want a cigarette at any time, please just ask, it's not an inducement though, is that understood?"

"I am as anxious as you are to clear this up."

"All right then, when you spoke to the officers at Harrogate you made certain admissions to them. I am not going to refer to what you said specifically, I want to hear what you have to say today, to us."

Jenkins nodded, "That's fine by me."

"Tell me about Mrs Sanders, how and why you killed her and what you did with her?"

"She was a lovely old lady and was staying in the hotel that I had been living in for quite a few years. I got to know her over the years and we had several meals together or a drink either before or after dinner. I am not a big drinker, I just enjoyed her company."

"Why her then, this, as you described her, this lovely old lady?"

"I was desperate for cash. She came to me with a rather silly idea for making plastic fingernails and I thought that it might be a way to get her to my place in Leeds and dispose of her."

"Is that the annex you rented from Mr Dean, on Black Bull Street?"

"Yes, it's where they all took place."

"Before we come onto them, can we concentrate on Mrs Sanders please?"

"Sorry, I'm getting ahead of myself. A few days ago, I picked her up and took her to Leeds. I opened up, led her inside and hit her on the head with a piece of piping."

"Where is this piece of piping?"

"I usually put it back on the shelf behind the door."

"Then what?"

"I took off all her clothing, apart from her undergarments, rolled her into an oil drum, then pumped the acid into the drum, once I had managed to stand it up. It was quite a strain I have to tell you, she was quite a large lady."

"What was the purpose of that?"

"It would dissolve her."

"You thought that you were on safe ground then because of your understanding of what Corpus Delicti meant then?"

"Fireproof, I suppose you could say. I have made a very big mistake haven't I?"

"What did you do with her once you thought that she had been dissolved?"

"Poured the remains away outside, it was perfect for that. Have you been?"

"Yes we have, we spent some time there, mainly inside though."

"And the money would come from where, exactly?"

"I would sell the fur coat, once it was cleaned. I had already pawned her jewellery."

"I mean the real money, this would only get you a few hundred pounds unless I am mistaken?"

"Oh, I see what you mean. In the long term, or as soon as I could, I would have sold off what she had in the way of investments and property. I knew that she was quite wealthy."

"How would you have done that?"

"At school, I called it copying but it's actually forgery. I am rather good at it, without blowing my own trumpet; I have had a lot of practice. I would have forged things like

Powers of Attorney letters, letters to solicitors, that sort of thing."

These detectives sat dumfounded, unable to comprehend the magnitude of what this man sat opposite them was telling them.

"I realised though that I had not thought it through enough. She was too close to home; it wouldn't take long for the finger of suspicion to start pointing in my direction. That is what happened of course. I owed a lot of money, desperate actually."

It was now the turn of Les Stead to ask a question,

"Who to, who did you owe money to? We know that you were behind on the hotel account, who else?"

"Bookmakers is the simple answer. I owed them an awful lot of money, my credit was always good, but they were making final demands. There were veiled threats of violence towards me, I had to come up with some money. It sounds very callous, but that's what the money would have been used on and for my lifestyle in general, living in an hotel is expensive you know."

"How much did you think you would get from Mrs Sanders' estate?"

"I had no real idea, I didn't get that far, she had all the trappings of wealth and I know that her husband left her well provided for. She told anyone that would listen to her that."

"Did you have what we would call a proper job or a profession? I have seen your business card, and that says that you are an engineer, is that true?"

"Alas no, I wish I was, I used to dabble a bit, doing small repairs to things."

"I'm sure we will cover that later."

"Did you ever do any repairs or engineering work of any description in Hunslet?" (Referring to the annex).

He hesitated and asked for a cigarette.

"What was the point, no."

" Let me put that another way. Was the sole purpose of you renting what you called your "factory" for you to kill and then dispose of your victims?"

"Would there be any chance of some more tea please?"

"Yes there would, we could do with some as well."

He asked to go to the toilet, escorted by DC Stead there and back. The trio sat in silence for a short while. He took up his position as before and the interview recommenced.

"You have had a while to ponder over what I asked a short time ago, can you answer the question?"

"Well, it is difficult for me to explain; in my head, I have never used the expression "killing them.""

"Mr Jenkins, Nick, if it pleases you, with regard to Mrs Sanders. You hit her on the head with a metal bar and she fell to the floor, is that correct?"

"Yes I told you that and it's true."

"Was she dead? Did you check for a pulse?"

"Yes I did and yes she was."

"Isn't that killing her?"

"If you put it like that I suppose it is, I just don't like the phrase, that's all."

"Does the word upset your sensibilities?"

Jenkins paused, "It does actually."

"I am not going to play word games with you, we have a long way to go," the inspector continued.

"So you, and you alone, let me be in no doubt, were responsible for her death; she didn't die of heart failure did she or old age, or did she when she saw where you had taken her?"

Burton realised at once that his use of sarcasm might

have provided an escape of sorts; it was a silly thing to ask him, and potentially damaging.

"Oh yes, it was me I was totally responsible."

Having established the salient points regarding the death of Mrs Sanders, some time was spent on discussing his upbringing and his life in general terms. Although his previous convictions were not admissible as such, his time in HMP Lincoln was entirely relevant with regard to his first use of acid. His avoidance of conscription was also talked about, it did not go down well, nothing of what he said did. He was likeable enough but secretly they both despised him. They had to maintain professionalism though, at all times, this was a huge case and it was about to get bigger...

"Didn't you worry that Mr Dean would come and see what you were up to?"

"No, he said quite categorically that he would not come round, he had no need to, besides, I saw him socially. Or rather his daughter more than him."

He went into a lot more detail regarding what, on the face of it to the officers, was a very strange relationship. Jenkins though seemed to be breaking the mould as far as strange was concerned.

"How did you obtain this acid?"

"A local firm, almost directly opposite, they delivered it when I needed it. I started an account with them and always paid it on time."

"Did they take it inside for you?"

"No, I met them outside. They would deliver almost at once for me and it was the same with the drums too, I'm sure you want to know that as well don't you?"

"The same company?"

"Not too far away."

Jenkins provided the contact details and addresses of

both these suppliers and the pawnbrokers he had used, and in due course statements would be obtained from them. Initially, the drum manufacturer was loathe to provide any information. The owner said that he could see the headlines "Drums of Death" in the papers. He was given an assurance that as far as possible their name would be left out of any proceedings, as was the manufacturer of the deadly liquid. But there could no guarantees.

"Shall we start at the beginning? The beginning of this series of murders? Is it fair to say that you killed them all for financial gain, to have what they had? You specifically chose wealthy people?"

"I suppose so, if you look at it like that."

"What other way is there to look at it?" asked Les Stead.

"Shall we start then?"

Jenkins then told the officers about the Nortons, all three of them. They sat, transfixed to their chairs.

"If I could, I would apologise to the Nortons, all of them."

"Why is that," Burton asked.

"I really liked Jack Norton, I had already made my mind up to dispose of him, but when he talked about wanting to avoid conscription it seemed to fall into place for me."

"So it was his fault that you killed him was it?" Stead could not resist asking this question.

"No, of course not, but if truth be told I was looking forward to the challenge, he was the first."

"That strikes me as extremely arrogant, are you an arrogant person Nick?"

"No I would not describe myself as arrogant. I'm sorry if it comes across like that but it's hard to explain."

"We are listening Nick, it's what we do," the Inspector added.

"May I have another cigarette please?"

It was lit for him, he placed it between the first and second fingers of his right hand, and paused, taking a moment.

"I'm not proud of what I did, but you see, I thought of it as business, if you can understand that?"

"In a word, no, and I think that I speak for both of us when I say that we have never heard anything like this and I doubt whether anyone else has," the detective inspector said.

Les Stead nodded his head in agreement and asked Jenkins, "Nick, there are just the three of us in here, is what you are telling us the truth?"

"Oh yes officers, why would I make it up?"

"If you were mad you might, criminally insane?"

"Why? Do you think that I might be?" Jenkins countered with his almost compulsory wry smile.

Stead continued without replying.

"At Harrogate Police Station you asked one of the detectives about Broadmoor, why was that?"

"I was just making conversation with him."

"No you weren't, you actually called him back and asked him specifically about it, didn't you?"

"Look, I am in a very difficult position, put yourself in my shoes."

Burton interrupted, "Are you saying, in spite of the fact that you have told us that you are not insane, that it was all business, that madness will be your defence to these matters?"

"I would rather not say at this stage; that will be up to other people, not me."

The officers let the matter ride, it was up to other people, certainly not them right now.

This was a real life horror story but Jenkins was so, so, matter of fact about this and the others that would follow. It was hard not to show any emotion, he was talking about killing human beings in what sounded like a scientific experiment. Frankenstein in reverse. Jenkins was no man of science, no writer of a classic novel; he was an out and out killer.

"What about P.E.L. then, the initials on the cigarette case and the attaché case? Who was he?"

"That was Dr Learoyd and his wife Alice. He was a doctor up in Middleham. Peter Edgar Learoyd to be precise."

"Is that Middleham with the castle where Richard the Third lived?" interjected Les Stead, showing off his historical knowledge, Eddie would say later over a pint.

"Beautiful part of the country, I went there a lot looking for racing tips."

"Did you get any?"

"Not really, I thought I knew better than they did, the odd one came through."

"Did the pistol belong to him?"

"It did, I took it out of their house after dinner one evening and after they had all had a bit too much to drink and were a bit distracted by it. He showed it to me as a trophy of war. I was going to use it on them but I had never fired a gun in my life and besides, it was very heavy, the bullets could have gone anywhere and made a lot of noise too. He was rather a show off, especially when he had too much to drink."

"Did you kill them in the same way?" Burton asked but anticipating the answer.

"Yes one after the other like Mr and Mrs Norton, I got

them there on some pretext or other, I forget what it was now."

"Forgive me, but I need to know this, wasn't this a dangerous thing to do or is that what you used the gas mask for? I nearly passed out when I stirred the bottom of one of the drums and that was a long time after anyone had been in it presumably?"

"When I put Jack Norton in the oil drum, the first one, I nearly passed out from the fumes so I had to get some form of protection. I had not done it before and didn't know what to expect. I bought the stirrup pump, the rubber gloves and apron."

"Can you remember the name of the shop where you bought them from or was it different ones?"

"Different ones in Leeds and in Wakefield, I could show you but I can't remember the names of them, sorry."

There was a knock at the door, "Come in," the inspector said. A young constable put his head around the door, "There's a message for you sir, they said it was urgent."

"We will have a break now whilst I go and see what this is, ok?"

"Thank you"

He was taken back to his cell, given a jam sandwich and the watch on him resumed as before.

The two detectives came out of the interview room and looked at each other, initially without speaking. They were lost for words, again.

"What do you make of that Eddie?"

"I have no bloody idea, but it has to be true doesn't it, no one could make that up could they? He had all the stuff, the acid, the drums and all the paraphernalia."

"That's what I think too, but does he have anything up his sleeve? I don't think that he's mad, he's not saying he is or screaming for a psychiatrist. Can you remember what Veronica does for a living?

"Hang on a minute; doesn't she work in a hospital?"

"We will ask him that when we deal with whatever this message is about."

The message was from the crime scene. It was from the pathologist, Dr Turvey; he wanted to see them as soon as possible.

A car took them, and would wait until they were finished. "Good news gentleman" the doctor started with, "I have found something that may interest you, and it certainly interests me."

In a metal kidney dish that he retrieved from inside his official vehicle were two items, one they recognised at once, the other one, or rather the other two, they had never seen before. The first was a pair of false teeth, which were self-explanatory, and the other small items resembled cherry stones.

"Right then, as far as the teeth are concerned we should be able to identify those, I think they are fairly new and are probably made from a sort of acrylic substance. Did this Mrs Sanders, was it, wear false teeth?"

"Don't know but we can find out, what are the little stones then?"

"They are the key to this I think, as far as you are concerned. I knew from her brief medical history that she suffered with gallstone problems, and these are gallstones. They probably never would dissolve."

"Can we say with certainty that they are hers?"

"Not with certainty, but it's all about the odds sometimes, what are the chances of finding them in this stuff if they are not hers? Granted it's circumstantial but it's evidence none the less."

The pathologist was very experienced and had heard it all at court.

"Wait till his legal people have finished with him, now I must press on. Lots to do."

He continued probing and the two went back to the police station, but not without the piece of lead piping left exactly where Jenkins had said it would be.

A telephone was the first stop in their own office. They contacted their colleagues in Harrogate and asked them to make urgent inquiries regarding the teeth.

Jenkins was brought back into the interview room, the officer who came back with him said that he had had a nap, not a care in the world, slept like a baby.

"Are you always this relaxed Nick? You've just had a sleep haven't you?"

"If I am being honest, and I hope that I am, I am enjoying getting this off my chest, it is a relief."

How many times had officers, in interview situations, told their suspects exactly this?

"Get it off your chest you'll feel better."

It usually sounded clichéd. But here we had it, the roles were almost being reversed. He sounded too good to be true. They tried another tack.

"Nick? Do you realise what a serious situation you are in, actually it couldn't be more serious?"

"I am trying to come to terms with it, I have made a terrible mistake," a wry smile came onto his face yet again, it seemed to be his default facial expression.

"This Corpus Delicti really will be the death of me won't it?"

A wry smile came across the faces of the policemen this time which almost turned, but not quite, into full blown laughter. Whatever faults he had, and he seemed to have many, lack of a sense of humour didn't appear to be one of them.

Les left the room and returned a short while later wearing a pair of leather gloves and in his gloved hands he held the lead piping.

"Is this it? Is this what you hit them and killed them with?"

"It looks very much like it, was it where I said it would be?"

The question was treated almost rhetorically and not answered directly. (Fingerprint analysis would reveal partial prints from Jenkins' right hand, good enough for court).

"To sum up then Nick, it was about the money, you killed these six totally innocent people so that you could live the high life and if it went wrong you could use this "Corpus Delicti", as you understood it, to get you out of it, planned, clinical murders, is that about right?"

"When you say it like that then yes, that's why I did it."

Chapter 39

PAPERWORK NOW HAD to be completed; "two-fingered typing" sorted out the charge sheet and later that evening he was charged with the murder of Mrs Amelia Sanders. He would appear at Leeds Magistrates Court the next morning when a remand in custody would be applied for.

Harrogate got back to them with some good news from Mrs Da Luca, she had identified which dentist Mrs Sanders had used and the teeth were despatched, with a police officer, for continuity of evidence, to this dental practice in the town. They would be examined the next day.

Dr Turvey had not found anything more specifically but was arranging to transport hundreds of pounds of the sludge to whichever laboratory was capable of handling it. He needed to know, as he suspected that it had once been human remains. He would also conduct a rough field test for the presence of sulphuric acid in the sludge which would be positive.

In due course, the best that the forensic scientists were

able to come up with was that it contained human fat residue and traces of the acid. No further specific identification would ever be possible. More evidence of a circumstantial nature.

This part of it was over; Alf Barker had told them to see him in their local pub when they had sorted the paperwork out. A debrief, if you like, over a couple of pints. It was what they always did. They were mentally exhausted and physically tired. It had been a long day and a day they would never forget. Six murders, but not just any old murders. Long after he had retired Eddie Burton would give a talk about this at the Regional Detective Training School.

They talked and talked, analysed until they could analyse no more. As closing time beckoned, Detective Superintendent Barker rang the station and arranged for the night detective to collect them and take them home, although Les was within walking distance. They would have to be back in the morning at 8am for another intense day.

Back at Dewsbury Road, the press had started to gather outside; another leak to them, this was not on. The 4pm briefing only told them what most of them already knew. They were told that a man would appear at court in the morning charged with murder. That was the official line but they wanted more, they always did, it sold newspapers after all.

Jenkins asked if could have a wash and shave. The first part was easy but he would have to be rigorously supervised for the second part of his request. A Gillette safety razor was provided to that end. He was "fed and watered" and put to bed for the night. Not only was the door open but the light was left on. He would have to get used to that. He tried to make small talk with the officer outside his door until it was made clear that that was not his purpose for being there.

Shift changeover came at 6am the next day with a fresh face for Jenkins to look at. It was a boring but extremely important job to do; this particular officer was new in service. A breakfast of sorts, another jam sandwich and a tin mug of tea, was offered and accepted. Apart from the quality of the food, he had no complaints; he had been treated well.

The press were back, should they try a decoy to put them off? It was decided not to. He would be put in the back of a van, a "Black Maria" as they were colloquially called. It had no side windows but two on each of the rear doors.

As they drove out of the archway gate the sound of popping flash bulbs filled the air. The journey time to the Leeds Bridewell was no more than ten minutes. He was put into a holding cell and would remain there until the case was called.

There was no application for bail from a solicitor acting on his behalf and chosen at random from a list. The magistrates remanded him in custody for one week and he was taken to HMP Leeds in Armley.

The remands continued week by week until he was committed, after a full committal hearing, for trial at the next Leeds Assizes. The weekly visits to court then ceased, no more "days out". He was now in the custody of the Prison Service and the Crown.

He was their total responsibility and held in the remand wing of this very old prison. Every move he made would be supervised. He wrote to his parents but asked them not to visit him. They had no intention of seeing

him, and they never did, not even in court. They had no
son; the embarrassment had almost destroyed them. They
did, however, write to him; until the very end they wrote
to him.

Chapter 40

When I arrived at Leeds Prison after I had been remanded in custody, my world was coming to an end. I realised that, so I had to make the best of a bad thing.

I was taken to the remand wing to start with like all the other unconvicted inmates. I was in a cell with one other person. He was raving mad and talked to himself all the time. I had thought of watching him to see if I could use that as some sort of defence.

Would my knowledge of what Veronica had told me work? That was why I had asked her about it in the first place. In case of a rainy day. It was throwing it down and I needed it. I had to pretend to be schizophrenic, that was it. I had a good knowledge, or thought that I had. I tried to get a book out of the prison library on diseases of the mind but they didn't have one.

The food was dreadful but I had to eat. After many years of smoking, going to a shop and buying the cigarettes of my choice in a packet, I had to get used to smoking "roll ups". This was the only useful thing my cellmate would do for me. He made me a supply of hand-rolled cigarettes every day. I gave him some for his trouble.

I was seen by my solicitor and I gave him what I thought was my defence strategy. It was either that or plead guilty. I was fighting for my life and couldn't do that. On the second or third occasion that he came to see me he told me that he had found a suitable psychiatrist who would be coming to see me, which indeed he did.

I got used to the regime in the prison, but never got used to the noise, especially at night. I was bored out of my mind. I tried to read but I couldn't concentrate at all. We were taken outside in all weathers for exercise whilst the Screws stood in the corners wearing waterproof clothing. The periods of activity in this prison and all the prisons that I had been in are called "association". The best activity was "ping pong". Not for me though I just sat and talked to anyone who wanted to talk. It was all nonsense really, nothing too serious. Not for the want of trying, I have to say; they did not seem to be aware of world events that I had kept up to date with outside. A lot of them had been in the War, which was a subject I could not and would not talk about. Someone did ask me what I did in the War so I lied and told him that I had a bad heart. I was tempted to say I was not expected to live much longer but I didn't want to tempt fate.

There were some very unsavoury characters in there, as you might expect. For some reason I was never bothered by them. Fights were commonplace, mainly over tobacco.

It was then time to see the medical men; the prison psychiatrist was the first to see me. Dr Brown. I was taken to the prison hospital wing, where his office was. He had worked in this establishment for a very long time and it showed. He was openly hostile towards me when he found out I was basing my defence on insanity. He did all the tests. Had I fallen out of a tree as a child? His parting shot was that there was nothing wrong with me and I was trying to pull the wool over his eyes. He actually called me a malingerer. My man, Dr Aspinall, came next. He had been found for me by my defence solicitor, with his fee being paid by the News of the World. He seemed to be quite sympathetic to my predicament but he was hard to read. He was more of an academic than a psychiatrist, in private practice.

I had all the same tests done again, but he kept his findings to himself as he said he would be doing a report and would no doubt be giving evidence at my up and coming trial which was getting ever nearer. He did not instil me with any confidence at all. If he was the best then God have mercy on my soul…

Chapter 41

Since 1864, Leeds, in common with other large cities, had held its own Courts of Assize, the Assizes, the highest tier of criminal trials, in the country.

The Assizes in Leeds were held in the Town Hall, a magnificent edifice constructed to celebrate the visit of Queen Victoria to the town, as it then was, prior to it receiving city status.

Leeds formed part of the North Eastern Circuit and from time to time had visiting judges.

On this day, Monday 24th January 1949 the visiting judge was no lesser a personage than the Lord Chief Justice, Lord Andrew Sinclair-Ross. Ross had been in post for the last four years and was both revered and feared in equal measure. That he was a dispenser of justice, there was no doubt. In his day he had been an outstanding advocate, specialising in prosecuting. He used to love the cut and thrust of cross examinations, a claim that many made, but Ross really did enjoy it. He was now in his early seventies and had followed a traditional route into law. A minor public school then Oxford, and was called to the bar in 1900. He was appointed a King's Counsel, (KC), taking silk as it was called, in 1920.

It was rumoured, more than rumoured in fact, that he had asked for this particular case.

Court No.1, on the ground floor, was full to capacity. Unlike the Central Criminal Court in London, better known as The Old Bailey, where seats could be bought and sold, this court was strictly first come, first served. The public gallery was, in the main, middle-aged ladies. The reporters, almost sat on top of each other, had their own gallery.

The minute hand on the Potts and Co. clock approached the hour of ten o'clock. It did not strike the hour; it was seen but not heard. A side door opened and in walked the Lord Chief Justice of England. Resplendent in a black robe with a broad red sash and a full, long white wig fashioned from horsehair. Such were the traditions of the English legal system.

In the well of the court, opposing counsel were in place, surrounded by bundles of papers. They too, wore robes and white wigs.

For the Crown: Mr Bernard Lazenby KC together with his junior, Mr Donald Jefferson.

For the defence: Mr Richard Stevens KC and alongside him, Mr Frederick Johnstone.

The term "Junior Counsel" was somewhat misleading; it was their job in court, usually, to ask questions of the "lesser" witnesses in order of their importance. In the case of Mr Johnstone, he was actually older than Mr Stevens, neither he nor Mr Jefferson had taken "silk" but they were nonetheless important cogs in the wheels of justice that were just about to start turning. Behind them were instructing solicitors, the go-betweens.

All that was missing now was the defendant.

"Put up Nicholas Jenkins," the also bewigged clerk of the court bellowed.

Jenkins appeared from the holding cells deep below this courtroom. As he walked up the closed staircase he was accompanied by two prison officers who stood at either side of him when he was upright, and sat whenever he was allowed to. All three of them remained upstanding as the clerk read out the only charge on the indictment:

"Nicholas Jenkins, you are charged that you, on or about the 14th January 1949, did wilfully and with malice aforethought murder Amelia Sanders contrary to Common Law. How say you?"

He stood directly opposite the judge and with his hands gripping the metal railing that surrounded the dock he replied, "Not Guilty my Lord".

Chapter 42

JENKINS WAS WEARING A LOVAT GREEN, single-breasted three-piece suit; a white shirt and a maroon tie completed his attire. The usual pencil-slim moustache adorned his top lip and his side-parted hair was slicked back with Brylcreem that had been provided by his solicitor downstairs, as had the tie.

He was motioned to sit down by his uniformed companions, and did so.

The jury, which would be all male, would soon be empanelled. One of the potential jurors was excused because he did not believe in capital punishment; another one on some obscure religious grounds. They took their places on the handmade oak benches on two levels, one behind the other. Comfort did not feature in their welfare, as cushions to sit on were not provided. These were seats to concentrate the mind and to keep you awake.

His Lordship outlined the proceedings to the jury and took great care in informing them of their onerous responsibility. Just below where he sat the shorthand writer, using the system devised in the 19th Century by Isaac Pitman, sat at a small table.

A wooden dais was in front of Mr Lazenby upon which rested more papers. On the bench directly behind him was a clerk with a pencil that was poised to write down everything that he said. He started to speak and his voice almost echoed. The case for the prosecution was expected but instead he asked his Lordship for permission to make a legal submission.

What was this? The trial was not yet under way and here we are asking for a submission. Surely, for whatever reason, the charge was not going to be dismissed, with Jenkins free to go?

Mr Lazenby had pre-warned the judge, and the defence, what his intentions were going to be, but it had to be done formally. There was no need to worry on that score; his submission concerned the other five murders. He wanted to introduce and use what is known as "Evidence of Similar Facts". In lay terms it meant that evidence could be produced to help prove that Jenkins in this case had committed almost identical crimes and this would help prove the crime that he was on trial for.

This legal strategy had been used before. Perhaps the most famous example was at the Old Bailey in 1915. George Joseph Smith was on trial for his life too. He had married a woman bigamously and then it was alleged that he murdered her in a bathtub by drowning her. He was given the sobriquet, "The Brides in the Bath Murderer" by the newspapers of his day. It had transpired that he was probably responsible for the murders of two others in almost identical circumstances. Similar Facts Evidence was allowed and without doubt led to a very speedy guilty verdict. Smith was duly executed. Smith of course was

Jenkins' most visited effigy in the Chamber of Horrors at Madame Tussauds.

Lazenby could have used this as a precedent but in the event, had no need to. The judge asked the jury to leave the court whilst this submission was taking place.

The learned barrister outlined his proposals which were compelling arguments. The defence, trying to make a show of it to Jenkins no doubt, tried a series of at best half-hearted objections. They were walking on legal quicksand.

The Lord Chief Justice allowed the submission and the jury regimentally walked back in to court. Jenkins, who had listened to all of this, sat in the dock looking impassive.

The trial could now start in earnest. It was scheduled to last three days.

Chapter 43

LAZENBY INFORMED his honour and the jury as well, of course, that some witnesses would not be called to give evidence. This was because both the prosecution and the defence had accepted what they would have to say, or had already said, in the form of written statements. Nonetheless these statements would be read out to the court and would be delivered by Mr Jefferson in due course.

"This case, members of the jury, is in my opinion, and I hope yours too, quite straightforward. I will endeavour to prove to you that the prisoner, Jenkins, was guilty of a total of six murders."

He explained to them what the legal submission had been about, in layman's terms, so that they would have no trouble understanding why this man was only charged with one murder but all six would be talked about.

"This case will be talked about, written about, long after we are gone; such is the magnitude of it. In all my days at the Criminal Bar, I have never come across anything like it, never heard anything like it. You may well think the same. It is my task and that of my learned junior counsel, Mr Jefferson, to prove guilt in this case beyond a shadow of doubt. That is our responsibility and it is an arduous one, as is yours of course. Mr Stevens and Mr Johnstone will try to prove the opposite, that Jenkins is not guilty beyond a reasonable doubt."

"One of the many links of commonality, and there are a lot, is that they: Mr Jack Norton, his parents, Mr and Mrs Norton, Dr and Mrs Learoyd and Mrs Amelia Spencer all disappeared without trace but, in the case of Mrs Sanders, not entirely without trace as I hope to prove later.

"After these entirely innocent and good people were murdered, he," he, to emphasise the point, pointed to Jenkins sat in the dock. "He plundered their bank accounts and sold properties to realise their assets by forging an array of documents. The fur coat that Mrs Sanders wore on her last journey was not safe from his clutches either. After he had killed her, he took it to a dry cleaning business to have it cleaned in order to sell it. He did not get that far."

"All the Nortons' properties were sold after many years of building up a very successful property rentals business. All of the proceeds went straight into his pocket, nowhere else, to feed his living the high life without having to work for it. Work, gentlemen of the jury, that you and I do at least five days a week, every week. To him it was an anathema, a four letter word."

He went on to describe what other things Jenkins had realised from the lives and deaths of his victims. The cars, how he had cultivated Mrs Sanders over the years, in spite of living under the same communal roof. He talked about the Learoyds in a similar vein. He even mentioned the massive coincidence that the Nortons and Learoyds were friends. It lasted for an hour and a half. He painted a very dark picture in his opening address, a very dark picture.

It was now the turn of the defence to open. Mr Stevens was on a hiding to nothing, in effect he was trying to defend the indefensible.

"Members of the jury, you have heard what my learned friend Mr Lazenby has said in his opening address to you. Usually, I would try to tell you that what he had said never took place. I am not going to do that, what I am going to do is say my client did carry out these truly atrocious crimes. The evidence, circumstantial in the main it may be, is overwhelming."

There was a murmur around the court that grew louder, was he trying to do the work of the prosecution? It sounded like it. The murmur died down as he resumed.

"Part of the job of the defence is to ensure that justice is carried out, and I'm sure that His Honour would agree with that."

He looked up at the judge, but if he was looking for any sign of agreement, he was out of luck. "To that end, the defence in this case will be to show you, to prove to you, that my client at the time of each and every one of these horrendous crimes was insane. He did not know what he was doing according to the M'Naghten (pronounced McNaughton) Rules. I will be calling a very eminent psychiatrist on behalf of my client," he looked at the dock, "Mr Jenkins."

"I will leave the explanation of what I have just told you to the psychiatrist, it is, after all, his field, not mine."

He then talked at length about his client, his upbringing and his life in general. It was not a long address to the jury. He did not want to bore them. By anyone's standards, he was waffling.

The prosecution introduced the accepted statements. Read out to the court by Mr Jefferson they were as follows:

Mr Douglas Dean, as the owner of the annex.

A Mr Fox, on behalf of Leeds Chemicals, the suppliers of the sulphuric acid.

Similarly, a Mr Evans, on behalf of Hunslet Fabrications, the manufacturers of the oil drums.

Three assistants from pawnbrokers shops.

Miss Hackett and Mrs da Luca from the Isola Bella Hotel.

Other ancillary statements were read, including a statement from the police officer who delivered the "teeth" to the dentist in Harrogate and from a forensic scientist who helped to prove that the "sludge" from the scene had in fact been human fat.

The day in court was ending after this business and the judge intimated that the court would be adjourned for the day. He rose, bowed, and the barristers did likewise in his direction as a mark of respect to him. Sedately, His Honour left the courtroom. On the other hand, the reporters looked like Olympic sprinters; they could not get out of the court quickly enough. Eager to find the nearest telephones to file the stories of the day's events, eager to have the biggest headlines in the morning newspapers.

Jenkins was taken down the stairs and thence back to prison for the night. The barristers adjourned to their robing room to take off their wigs and gowns. A five-minute walk would take them to the Hotel Metropole where rooms for them had been reserved. Perhaps a rest, perhaps planning for the next day.

Chapter 44

WITHOUT THE CEREMONY TO mark the opening of the Assizes, R-v-Jenkins began its penultimate day. All the main players took their places as this drama headed towards a crescendo.

Mr Fitzgerald called Dr Turvey, the forensic pathologist.

He was led through his evidence without needing to be prompted, as some even professional witnesses have to be. He was articulate and spoke in a language that the jury would understand. After telling the court about his qualifications, he described the scene he had come across, the grid system for searching that he had devised and so on. The photographs of the scene spoke thousands of words and copies were handed to the jury.

Fitzgerald asked him about the gallstones.

"Dr Turvey? Were you expecting to find these items? Were you at all surprised?"

"I have never come across any gallstones before that were not within the confines of a human body."

"A dead body would that be doctor?"

"Yes, but in this particular case I had been informed that the missing lady had a history of problems associated with them, so I was not altogether that surprised."

Mr Fitzgerald asked the clerk of the court to pass him a covered glass Petri dish from the exhibits desk which he asked to be handed to the doctor stood in the witness box.

"Are these they?"

"Yes they are, they have my signature on the label."

As he held them, they rolled around in the dish like very small marbles that children played with.

"Goodness they are small aren't they?" asked Fitzgerald. "Please pass them to the jury." The jury members looked at them and they were put back on the table.

"Can I show you the teeth now please? You found these in the search as well, is that correct?"

"Yes that's correct; they have an identification mark on them showing who the manufacturer was."

"Why didn't they dissolve, do you think, in your expert opinion?"

"They are made from an acrylic resin. I actually did an experiment in my lab and after two weeks they, not these ones of course, had not dissolved."

"In sulphuric acid?"

"Yes"

"You also removed, or arranged to have removed, an awful lot, a huge amount of what can only be described as sludge, did you not? What was the outcome of that examination?"

"Yes indeed Your Honour, we did, the best we came up with was that it was human fat, it was not possible to disseminate it any further. It was without any shadow of doubt human fat."

"How much fat was there, in weight?"

"A total of 310 pounds in weight."

Fitzgerald added, in a theatrical whisper, "That's an awful lot of bodies."

If it was an attempt at humour, it failed although there was a snigger or two from the public gallery.

"Thank you Doctor Turvey, please stay there. Mr Stevens may have some questions for you."

Stevens stood after Fitzgerald sat. "No questions my lord," and promptly sat down again.

The evidence of identification of the false teeth was, at the last minute, accepted by the defence. The dentist had had a wasted journey.

In chronological order, the next witness was Detective Sergeant Nolan from Harrogate CID.

He, like the witness before and the witness afterwards, was led through his evidence. Jenkins sat appearing not to be paying attention at all. The cross examination by Mr Stevens was brief and succinct.

"What did you make of the "Corpus Delicti" matter? What was your reaction to when Mr Jenkins came out with it?"

"To be honest, sir, I was taken aback to say the least. I wasn't expecting it and neither was my colleague." Nolan went on to explain what had taken place and when asked to describe what this legal phrase meant, he did so for the benefit of the jury and the whole courtroom.

"Am I correct in saying that you explained what it actually means as opposed to what Mr Jenkins told you that it meant?"

"I did indeed sir, but we had to look it up first, to be legally accurate, so to speak."

Titters of laughter rang through the court but not enough for the judge to interject.

"So you are now an expert, would you say?"

"I am a police officer, not a barrister, although I will never forget this legal definition that's for certain."

"What was his, what was Mr Jenkins' demeanour like throughout your time with him?"

"He was extremely polite all the time."

"Did you think he could be insane?"

As soon as the words had left Stevens' lips, Fitzgerald was up as quick as a flash.

"My Lord."

The Judge was not having any of this, "Mr Stevens, you should know better than that, leave this to your psychiatrist."

"I apologise My Lord, it was a slip of the tongue and I will withdraw the question."

It was not a slip at all; it was a deliberate attempt to introduce his defence at the earliest opportunity. He continued asking the officer various other questions, trying to skirt around the insanity issue. Nolan was thanked and released; he sat behind the instructing solicitors.

"Call Detective Inspector Burton." Burton had been stood outside ready to enter. He extinguished a cigarette, fastened his suit jacket and walked towards the witness box. It was a path well trodden by him over the years.

The oath taken, he was ready to start. He had been looking forward to this, he didn't always enjoy giving evidence, few police officers actually did.

He gave his evidence in chief, which lasted an hour and a half. It covered everything from going to the annex, finding the oil drums and even the sneezing fit he had suffered, which caused some in the gallery to laugh, to finally charging Jenkins with the murder on the indictment. It painted a picture both of the scene and of Jenkins.

He was asked about the documentation regarding the forgeries, the banking information and so on.

"This was the most complicated and complex inquiry that I have ever worked on. Once he told us what he had done and why he had done it we had to start gathering evidence."

"In comparison to other murder inquiries that you have worked on, was it very different?"

"Yes sir, we started with almost nothing. We had papers from the Land Registry that showed what houses the Nortons had owned and what their son Jack Norton had owned.

"Once we established that we visited each and every property. We found that they were now owned either by individuals or by another property company."

"What was their reaction on finding this out?"

"Horrified, shocked and panicking as to whether they were the legal owners."

Trying to score some more sympathy, as if any more were needed, Fitzgerald continued,

"Was anyone actually made homeless as a result of these transactions?"

"Not as far as I am aware."

"Have you any knowledge of the legal position now with regard to the ownership of them?"

"As far as I am aware, the properties belong to the estate of the Norton family."

"And is there a Norton family?"

"None that we have managed to track down so far sir."

On final question, Inspector: "We have just mentioned that the Nortons did not have any family, was that the same for the others?"

"Yes sir it was and if I'm allowed to say, I don't think that it was a coincidence."

Although strictly speaking it was an opinion, it was one that the Inspector was allowed to have.

The cross examination would be over very quickly.

"Detective Inspector, how did you find Mr Jenkins?"

His Honour was not going down this road again, "Mr Stevens?"

"Oh no My Lord I didn't mean to imply…"

Cutting him off, the judge interrupted, stopping him in his tracks.

The next witness for the prosecution was to be Dr Brown, the prison psychiatrist. He entered the witness box and was wearing a brown three-piece suit, bought new for the occasion, it was said.

"Dr Brown," began Mr Fitzgerald, after he had taken the oath.

"Dr Brown, you are a very experienced psychiatrist are you not?"

"Yes My Lord, I have been qualified for over thirty years."

"And how long have you worked in prisons?"

"Almost twenty five of those years."

"On how many occasions did you consult, if that is the correct phraseology, with the prisoner in the dock, Jenkins?"

"On four separate occasions, that is usual in a capital case, and he was no exception."

"What was your diagnosis?"

"My diagnosis was, and still is, that there is nothing clinically the matter with him."

"So he is not mentally ill then? He knows the difference between right and wrong?"

"Indeed he does and no he is not, in my opinion, mentally ill."

"In your time in prison", which someone in the public gallery thought was funny. Fitzgerald rephrased the question.

"Dr Brown, during your time working as a prison psychiatrist, roughly how many examinations have you undertaken?"

"Thousands, Your Honour, I am kept very busy."

"I am sure that you are doctor. In laymen's terms, words the jury will understand, how would you, based on your huge experience of such matters, how would you describe him."

"He is a man totally without morals, he knows what he is alleged to have done is legally wrong and yet cares not a jot about it. He is in my view a psychopath, a narcissist and arrogant beyond the normal boundaries although that facet does not make into a person who takes lives."

"Did he tell you that he thought that he was a schizophrenic?"

"Yes he did, almost as soon as we met."

"Did you think that was strange, self-diagnosing a mental illness?"

"Very strange indeed."

"Can you remember the conversation? How it went?"

"It was something like, look here old boy I think I could save us both a bit of time, I think I am schizophrenic, or something very similar to that."

"And how did you react to that?"

"I was astonished, I thought that something wasn't right about this. No one has ever, and I mean ever, said anything like that to me before. It was as if he wanted me to agree with him straight off the bat, diagnose him then ship him off to Broadmoor or somewhere similar."

"Did he mention Broadmoor to you specifically"?

"Not specifically, no."

"It was an act then?"

"In my opinion, yes it was, this man, to reiterate, is not clinically insane in my opinion."

187

The next ten minutes or so were occupied by the psychiatrist being asked about the form that the examination took.

"Was he a pleasant person to deal with would you say?"

"He was but it is my job to strip off the veneer and see what lies beneath, this is what I believe I have done and my report says so."

"I am obliged to you doctor, please wait there, my learned friend may have some questions for you."

Mr Stevens rose from his seat holding a sheath of papers, sat back down again and then up in a flash.

"So then Dr Brown, in your opinion a man who kills six people and dissolves their bodies in acid is not criminally insane?"

"In my opinion Mr Stevens, not this man; four hours is a long time to spend with someone in my profession."

"Very well doctor, that is your opinion. I will be bringing a very eminent psychiatrist of my own to rebut your opinions. No further questions My Lord."

Chapter 45

It had been a long and productive morning for the Prosecution, and now, before it was the turn of the Defence, the court adjourned for lunch.

After lunch, Mr Stevens called Miss Veronica Dean as a character witness.

How would she fare in the witness box? As she approached it, she was already clutching a handkerchief.

"Thank you Miss Dean for coming today to court to tell us what you know about Mr Jenkins"

"You are saying that as if I had a choice, I do not want to be here, standing in front of all these people."

"I will try to be brief, but I cannot guarantee that my learned friend, looking across at Mr Fitzgerald, will be equally brief.

" When did you first meet Mr Jenkins?"

"When I was fifteen, nearly sixteen. He came to rent an old building my dad had to rent."

"How did he strike you?"

"He never hit me, never laid a finger on me, who told you that?"

His Honour entered the fray, not for the first time, "Choose you words more carefully Mr Stevens. I think what the counsel for the defence means, Miss Dean, is, how did he appear to you, did you like the look of him?" the judge interjected, putting Mr Stevens in his place.

"I am so sorry Miss Dean, that is exactly what I meant to say and I am obliged to his Lordship for pointing that out. An anomaly of the English language, where the same word can have different meanings."

"It is not an English lesson Mr Stevens, this is a court of law and your client is on trial for his life."

"I apologise My Lord and to Miss Dean as well."

"He looked like a businessman; he was well dressed and had a nice car."

"Is it right to say that a relationship developed between the two of you? And continued over the years?"

"Yes we became friends, but not like that if that's what you mean?"

"Miss Dean, the only relationship that I am suggesting is a platonic one, just good friends, that's all."

"That is what it was. When he took me to hotels we always had separate rooms."

"What did you think that he did for a living?"

"He was an engineer, that's what he told me. I had no reason to doubt it."

"How does it feel now, to see him stood there?"

She could contain her emotions no more and burst into floods of tears. Stevens stood, waiting for an answer, whilst she regained her composure which had been brittle to start with. The court seemed to be embarrassed for her apart from the reporters who were eagerly scribing away.

"It feels awful to see him like this, I did not know anything."

"I am not suggesting that for one moment you did.

Thank you Miss Dean, please wait there."

Fitzgerald had two questions for her:

"Miss Dean, did you have any idea where the money came from that he spent on himself and you?"

"No I did not, apart from his business."

"Am I correct in saying that you work as a secretary at a local hospital?"

"Yes sir, I do."

"And what is the specialism of the part of the hospital that you work in?"

"It's the psychiatric wing; I type reports and make appointments."

"Did Jenkins ever ask you about your work?"

"He used to, he was very interested in everything that I did."

"Anything in particular about what you did?"

"He asked me about schizophrenia, the symptoms and the cure for it."

"I do appreciate that you have no qualifications in psychiatry, but can you tell me what you understand by that?"

"It's a disease of the mind that involves people with split personalities."

"Thank you Miss Dean, I have no more questions and I am obliged to the court for allowing her to answer that question."

"My Lord, members of the jury, the only other witness for the defence is Dr George Aspinall."

This time the noise in the courtroom had to be quelled by the clerk. "Silence in court, silence in court." The noise, the gasps of astonishment, were subsiding but it took a while. They, members of both the public and the press galleries, felt short-changed. Jenkins would not give evidence!

Before Aspinall could take his place in the witness box, Fitzgerald continued, by way of an apology almost, "It is the right of my client to exercise his right not to give evidence."

"Are you Dr George Aspinall, a consultant psychiatrist?"

"Yes I am." He was dressed in a three-piece striped suit that looked to have seen better days in the opinion of some observers. He sported a yellow bow tie that gave him the appearance of an "Academic Don".

"Your qualifications please doctor?"

As he was part way into reeling off his long list of professional qualifications, the judge stopped him in his tracks.

"Thank you doctor, I have heard enough of those, I think I get the gist and so do the members of the jury."

Sinclair-Ross was not a fan of psychiatry or psychiatrists and it had only taken a moment to let that be known. He was very much "old school". To him this branch of medicine was all too new, not tried and tested enough for him.

"Dr Aspinall, may we start by you telling the court the legal definition of insanity?"

"Very well, it is a mental illness of such a severe nature that a person cannot distinguish between fantasy and reality due to his, in this case, psychosis or is subject to uncontrollable impulsive behaviour. They do not, cannot, differentiate between right and wrong."

"Thank you doctor for the explanation. I am sure we are all a lot wiser after that. Let me ask you about Mr Jenkins now. Where did you have you your consultations with him?"

"In a room at Leeds Prison."

"Just the two of you?"

"No, there was always a prison officer present on the grounds of safety you see."

"Yes I understand, how many times did you see him?"

"Oh, three or four times I think."

"Can you be more precise, it is important, how many times was it?"

He referred to his notes that were resting on the side of the witness box.

"Three times."

"And how long were these sessions for?"

"An hour each time."

A lot of time was taken up with psychiatry in general until the crunch questions had to be asked. Jenkins sat, seemingly ambivalent to what was going on around again.

"How did you get on with him?"

"Do you mean what did I make of him, what my conclusions were?"

"Yes I do, what conclusions did you come to? Does he fit the bill of the legal definition of insanity?"

"Well, I think that he does. I have carried out a lot of research on subjects and yes, I believe that he fits the legal definition."

"Thank you Dr Aspinall, please wait there."

Fitzgerald could not wait to begin:

"Three hours is not a long time to form conclusions like this is it?"

"I think it is, I am a very experienced psychiatrist."

"I am sure that you are. Tell me this though, what are your conclusions based on exactly?"

"Verbal testing."

"That is pretty standard," if he rose to the bait, he did not show it.

"Lots of tests are standard and I applied a lot of them to him."

A game of "cat and mouse," ensued between the two for some time. It ended, pretty much, as stalemate.

"Am I correct in assuming that you based your diagnosis on what he told you?"

"Yes of course."

"Did you ask him if he was a compulsive liar?"

"No."

"Why not, isn't that relevant to this?"

"I'm not sure what you mean?"

"Part and parcel of what this man, the accused in the dock, has done is tell a litany of lies throughout his entire life, of course it's relevant. He admitted he was a liar to just about everyone else afterwards, so why not you?"

"Because I didn't ask that direct question." Fitzgerald shook his head in a theatrical manner in the direction of the jury, as did the judge, but to himself.

"What psychosis does he suffer from?" asked the judge

"I'm not too sure; it may be an indeterminate one."

With more than a hint of sarcasm, which His Honour was well known for, he continued, "So if it's not in any of your text books how do you know for sure?"

"I can't be sure for certain, I just think he has one."

Mr Fitzgerald carried on, "On the same basis, that all this is based on what has come out of his mouth, don't you think it's more than a little bit possible that he has hoodwinked you?"

"It is possible of course."

"More than possible I would suggest. He is an out and out con man and a cold-blooded killer. How do you think con men earn a living Dr Aspinall?"

Fitzgerald knew he was on thin ice but the judge let him carry on.

"By telling lies?"

"Correct, by telling lie upon lie upon lie, just like he, pointing at Jenkins, has done for years."

"Doctor? Are you aware that Jenkins' friend Miss Dean worked in the psychiatric wing of a hospital as a secretary?"

"No, I did not know that."

"Furthermore, he used to ask her what schizophrenia was. Surely that was more than just idle curiosity in view of where we are now?" It was an almost rhetorical question.

"I did not know that."

"And the fact, and it is a fact, that whilst he was in custody at Harrogate Police Station he asked about how long he would have to serve in Broadmoor? A hospital for the criminally insane."

"I am not aware of that."

"You don't seem to be aware of very much Dr Aspinall."

He was a man on a mission now:

"By telling the lies he has done, could he have survived by not being able to tell the difference between right and wrong?"

"It's not that sort of right or wrong, it's not as easy as that, not as black and white."

"Not as black or white? Really? The whole purpose of that statement is that everybody knows exactly what it means. Jenkins is no exception, he has conned you doctor, conned you like all these victims."

"For the last time, did he in the accepted sense, the sense that the jury and all the people in this courtroom would understand and accept, know the difference between right and wrong? Yes or no?"

Aspinall hesitated for a moment, "Yes he did."

"No further questions My Lord."

"Mr Stevens?"

"No, My Lord, the defence rests."

It was approaching 4pm, His Honour adjourned for the day. Tomorrow would be the last day of this trial.

Without Jenkins giving evidence though, the trial did not develop into yet another so-called "Trial of the Century" that the newspapers had been looking forward to publishing a story about. In spite of that, it still occupied the headlines. It was still a "sensational story".

For one of them, The News of the World, who had paid for Jenkins' defence, their sales would increase dramatically in the weeks that his "story" was printed.

The trial now followed the way of all trials: closing speeches from the prosecution and the defence and finally the judge. Mr Fitzgerald reprised the evidence that the jury had heard over the previous two days. He almost ridiculed what the psychiatrist had told the court and asked them to find Jenkins guilty, guilty of capital murder.

Mr Stevens was on a hiding to nothing. He was just going through the legal motions, putting a show on, on behalf of Jenkins. He tried to repair the damage caused by the psychiatrist, but to no avail.

His Honour now summed up, instructing the jury on points of law and providing a fair, balanced view of the evidence. Where it was relevant and pertinent he would refer to passages of evidence, making sure they were in context. He, as the Lord Chief Justice, did not want to be criticised at the Court of Appeal. It was described as a fair summing up. The jury were sent out to deliberate and to take their time; there was no hurry, his Lordship told them.

There was an aura of anticipation in court, there always was when the life of a man was at stake. It was usually has he, or rarely she, done it? In this case that was never in doubt, he had done it, but was he mad?

An usher came in to the court, a message was whispered to the clerk of the court and he left the room. A verdict? Surely not? It was far too early, but a verdict had been reached. His Honour came into court flanked by a lay magistrate and a chaplain.

The jury took their places, the court was stilled and hushed. "Have you reached a verdict on which you are all agreed?" the clerk asked. The foreman rose from his seat, "We have My Lord."

"Do you find the prisoner at the bar guilty or not guilty of the only count on the indictment"?

"Guilty, My Lord."

"And that is the verdict of you all?"

"Yes My Lord."

The verdict had been reached in seventeen minutes…

It was time for the judge to take centre stage. As he said, "Stand up Jenkins," with the two prison officers standing simultaneously, there was a deathly silence throughout the court. No one spoke except His Honour:

"Nicholas Jenkins, you have been found guilty, and quite rightly in my opinion, of one of the most barbaric and heinous crime it has ever been my misfortune to hear. Have you anything that you wish to say before this sentence, the only one proscribed by law, is passed."

"Nothing at all," were the only words spoken by Jenkins other than when he had pleaded not guilty at the start of the trial.

He glanced to his left to the chaplain who, anticipating his duty, stood up and placed a black square of silk atop the judge's wig.

The sentence that ends, "And may God have mercy on your soul," was spoken.

"Take him down," were the last words that Jenkins heard in this court or any other…

Chapter 46

JENKINS LOOKED AROUND THE COURTROOM, looking for signs of recognition perhaps. Looking for the sympathy that would never materialise. He picked up his copy of the Daily Telegraph, provided by a clerk to his solicitor, the crossword almost completed.

He was tapped on the shoulder by one of the officers. It was time to leave. They set off to go down the staircase for the last time.

The steps seemed a lot steeper than on the way up. An officer at the front of him and one behind him. He gripped the handrail tightly and almost lost his composure, he did not want to let go of it.

From the key chain attached to his waist belt, one of the prison staff withdrew a key from his pocket. It was used to unlock a cell that he would be held in pending his journey back to prison. He was asked to take off his necktie, which he handed to the officers. He walked inside; it was beyond drab and he was beyond salvation. Nothing was said to him and he, never short of something to say, was not in the mood for talking. He did though ask for a cigarette. It was passed through the bars of the closed and locked gate, a match was struck and it was lit through the bars. The officers sat outside the cell on wooden chairs. Their eyes never left him. It was the start of a process that would see him watched over 24 hours a day until the end of his life.

Everything that he did, ate, read, even his toilet habits, would be recorded. From being an unconvicted prisoner on remand, with the few benefits that category had, was now a thing of the past. He had been elevated to the highest ranking in the prison system, not in the prison hierarchy, that of a condemned man. He asked how long it would be until they set off. It might be an hour, it might be longer.

In the distance and along a long corridor, Jenkins heard the sound of a gate being unlocked. Walking towards him he could see Mr Stevens, wig in hand, and his solicitor. He greeted Mr Stevens, "Thank you for everything you have done." Stevens asked for a consultation with Jenkins as he was allowed. The officers moved out of the way but the gate remained closed. Any conversation that took place was still covered by "privilege". The staff stayed out of earshot but within line of sight of the trio.

Mr Stevens took the lead and said, "I am truly sorry that we could not have done more."

They discussed an appeal. As it was a capital case, there was an almost automatic right of appeal. "On what grounds?" asked Jenkins. He continued, "It seems to me that I have been found guilty on the most overwhelming evidence, it was a fair trial. I am not mad, never was, and we both know that."

"I am sure that I can think of something, even if it just has the effect of delaying, you know, delaying…".

Jenkins jumped in. "Don't be afraid to say it Mr

Stevens, my execution… when they put the rope around my neck and hang me until I am dead."

"I didn't want to upset you," Stevens said.

Rather abruptly, Jenkins said, "I doubt whether you can."

One of the most useless sentences in the English language can be "try not to worry", but that is what Stevens said as he took his leave of Jenkins. The officers resumed their positions outside the cell.

He would never speak to or see Stevens again…

His wristwatch had already been removed too, but the effect of this was to cause him to ask what time it was, repeatedly.

An audible message was passed to his guards, as he referred to them; he didn't hear the exact content, but it was time to go, time to start the last chapter of his relatively short life…

He sat on one of the bench seats inside the prison van, handcuffed to one of the same two officers that had stood in the dock with him. The doors closed and a light switched on to provide some illumination. This would be the last time he would travel in any form of mechanised transport. It had been a day of lasts…

Chapter 47

THE PLAIN, black painted van reached its destination. It had only taken fifteen minutes. The driver, himself a prison officer, turned off the ignition and approached the main entrance of this huge and very austere building. Jenkins was, of course, no stranger to it.

The rear van door opened once inside the prison proper and Jenkins got out, still handcuffed. These "shackles" were taken off his wrists and he followed the driver to an inner office, the reception area of the prison. The staff were expecting him. It was too late in the day for normal admissions, but this was not a normal admission. More than ever before he was the property of the State.

Uniforms were everywhere, behind him, on the counter, and behind it stood two very burly officers. He recognised them from when he came in on remand. The uniform on the counter was earmarked for him. Unlike the clothes he was currently wearing, there would be no private fitting in Savile Row, no inside leg measurement taken. Grey woollen jacket and trousers and a blue and white vertically striped shirt were what his "new tailors" had provided. Bespoke it was not!

He changed clothes in full view of the staff and was searched, embarrassed or not, he had no choice. As he watched the suit and shirt that he had worn to court put in a brown paper bag, he asked what would happen to it. He did not get an answer. This ritual completed, one of the reception officers glared at Jenkins from across the counter, "Name?" Jenkins said to himself, "You know my bloody name," but kept quiet on the grounds of common sense and said, "Jenkins."

"Jenkins what?" barked the officer who appeared to be the most senior. A thought occurred to Jenkins that he might have been a Sergeant Major in a previous incarnation. Seeing as how Jenkins had managed to avoid any of the armed services during the war, he had no idea of what an actual Sergeant Major might sound or look like.

"Jenkins, sir", he shouted again.

"Jenkins sir", replied Jenkins.

"That's better lad, you have been on remand here so you know the ropes. You will refer to me and all my officers as sir or mister, do I make myself clear?"

"Yes, yes sir."

"Very well then, you will go with these officers who will take you to your new home. It's not the Savoy I'm afraid, but it's the best we have to offer and it comes with room service." The sarcasm was heavily accentuated. It stuck at the back of Jenkins' throat.

He was led away, gate after gate opened and closed behind him. Upstairs, along corridors until they reached his destination. On the way, he had been looking out for signs on closed doors that might have said, "condemned cell" or even "execution shed". He was out of luck and so would the casual observer have been.

The walls on the corridors were painted dark green up to the level of the tops of the cell doors when a drab yellowy paint took over, up to the ceiling. Ceiling lights were enclosed in metal grills. As ever, in all of the prisons he had been in, the floors were highly polished.

The cell that he would spend his last few weeks in had no such signs and neither did the "other room". They had reached a part of the prison that few people ever went. A thought occurred to Jenkins that he could not find his way back here again. He need not have worried on that score, he would not have to!

Chapter 48

THE DOOR WAS ALREADY OPEN a little and then fully opened in an outwards direction. The first thing he noticed was that there was an electric light in the centre of the ceiling protected by a metal grill. Although the bulb would be changed, he would never see this light turned off. He estimated that this room, his cell, measured about 12 feet square, or thereabouts. It was about 10 feet in height. Quite large by prison standards, he observed.

There was a single bed, bolted to the floor via metal legs, made up with a pillow minus a pillowcase, he noticed. The mattress looked a bit on the thin side for his liking, but was probably the same as in the remand wing. There was a wooden table with enough chairs to seat four people and an area that had a sink with a metal bucket underneath. He knew the purpose of the bucket, every cell he had been in had one. A green screen, to provide a modicum of privacy, looked a bit like it had come from a hospital, he thought. He would have been right.

· · ·

To HIS LEFT as he walked in was a large brown, wooden wardrobe that, when the time came, would be slid to one side to reveal the entrance to the execution chamber itself. If he knew this, he never gave it a thought. There was nothing else to see, apart from two prison officers who identified themselves to him.

Officers Davies and Ryan had come in early and would stay with him on this, his first night. They asked to be referred to as Mr Davies and Mr Ryan. Being the sociable person that he was, Jenkins offered his right hand to shake theirs. On the grounds of safety and propriety both of the men declined this offer.

No bond would ever be allowed to develop between Jenkins and whichever officers were on duty in his cell. They worked in two shifts, 7am until 7pm and 7pm until 7am. They used the same bucket as he did and ate what he ate. If they had views, any thoughts, on capital punishment they were instructed to keep them to themselves. Their job was quite simple, it was to keep Jenkins alive and unharmed. It was late in the day and they asked him if he was hungry; he just wanted a cup of tea and a cigarette.

He was up early the next morning before the officers changed over; Davies and Ryan were replaced by officers Jones and Nuttall. That was how it was. Sometimes other officers took their places when they were off duty, but in the main it was these four. It was felt that he, or anyone else in the position he was in, needed some sort of continuity.

After he had breakfast, the door opened. The officers suspected it might be the governor and their suspicions were correct.

"Good morning Jenkins, my name is Mr Dixon. This is my prison and my men are responsible for your welfare during your time with us. Just so you are in no doubt, the date for your execution is in three weeks, three weeks tomorrow in fact."

"My barrister has lodged an appeal," Jenkins replied. "That will give me some more time won't it?"

Dixon continued, "That may well be the case, and if that is so I will keep you informed, you have my word on that. You will be allowed access to the prison chaplain or any other person to see to your spiritual needs. Let my staff know. Do you have any questions?"

Jenkins asked the governor for permission to write what he called "some notes" to pass on to his legal people and would require some paper and something to write with. The governor, a decent human being it has to be said, could see no harm in this and allowed the request. Besides which it would help occupy Jenkins' mind and might, just might, take his mind off the inevitable date.

"Anything else?" Dixon asked as he was putting his key in the door. He was not expecting a question, but never in a million years did he expect what came next.

"Would it be possible, when the actual date is known, if the appeal fails, for us to have a rehearsal? You know, to make sure things go well on the day?"

"Trust me Mr Jenkins," Robert Dixon said, with an almost theatrical pause whilst reeling from the sheer arrogance of the man, "Trust me, Mr Jenkins, nothing will go wrong, you have my word on that too."

Chapter 49

THIS PRISON HELD prisoners on either remand, awaiting court appearances, or convicted prisoners sentenced for a variety of offences. Unlike the Dartmoors of this world, where prisoners had "hard labour" added to their sentences, Leeds Prison was regarded as hard without the "labour".

It was designed with a central hub with "wings" holding the prisoners in their cells radiating from the centre of the hub.

Colloquially it was known as "Leeds Castle".

It was, essentially, a local prison catering for Leeds and the West Riding of Yorkshire. Executions were rare, but in anticipation of it, the executioner and his assistant had been booked through the Department of Prisons at the Home Office.

Robert Dixon had been in post since 1946, he was fifty five years of age and had joined the department after War service in 1919. He attained the rank of Captain, and as such was entitled to use this title. He preferred not to as it might give him too much in common with his charges, many of whom were ex-servicemen. This would be his first execution, they did not happen too often in the provinces although Strangeways in Manchester had had a few. He had been trained in the protocol and was confident that things would go without a hitch. On a personal level, he was not a proponent of the death penalty but he would carry out his duties to the letter of the law.

He knew of Jenkins, who didn't? He knew what he been had been convicted of and the story behind the conviction. After the meeting with Jenkins, in a conversation with his wife at home, he described him as a cross between two characters from Dickens, Uriah Heep and Abel Magwitch, creepy and scary at the same time.

He did not like him one bit but he had to retain his objectivity at all times. As for the request for a "rehearsal", did he really think that would happen? What had he hoped to gain?

Was it simply an attempt at humour that failed, utterly failed…?

Dixon returned to his office and contacted the Department of Prisons at the Home Office to let them know all was well, as well as it could be bearing in mind this was his first execution, not forgetting that it was Jenkins' first as well, he allowed himself a smile.

It was a very busy prison and held just over a thousand inmates. He was busy all the time but he had three assistant governors under his command, all but one of them were ex-servicemen. That could be said of most of the officers. It seemed to be a natural progression after they had retired from whichever branch of the armed services they had served in, sixty per cent of them from the Army itself.

For many of the prisoners it was just like being back in the Army.

It was a disciplined environment, it had to be, and it started, for most of them, as soon as they arrived in this particular establishment when they were "greeted" by a former Sergeant Major in the Coldstream Guards.

There was a prison doctor as part of the staff and a hospital to deal with minor ailments. Any breaks of bones and anything remotely serious would be dealt with at one of the two local hospitals. It was like a conveyor belt sometimes and Dixon's staff had to accompany and stay with the "patient". It was a drain on manpower but it had to be done. For many of the officers it was a good source of paid overtime or time off in lieu.

Chapter 50

My RESEARCH HAD BEEN extensive but not exhaustive. People had long since died, but the relatives of the main players were extremely helpful, some, regretfully for my purposes, not so. Some taken from third hand accounts, no primary or even secondary sources existed anymore.

It is as accurate as I could make it.

I had, I thought, destroyed my relationship with Veronica. That was a bridge that could never be rebuilt.

Had it been worth it? Not really. Who did I think I was? The next Hemingway?

They had been aware of the parts that had been played, some small, some huge.

The court transcript was read and analysed, and for the sake of brevity, paraphrased as had all of the interviews.

Yet there was one account missing, one story that I needed from one of the most important players in this melodrama.

This person was alive…

Where did he live? How could I track him down? How

could I contact the man who for a generation or more, until his retirement, was known as the Chief Executioner, better known as the public hangman.

One of the last people, if not the last, to see and even speak to Nicholas Jenkins, albeit a one way conversation.

The problem was I had no idea how to contact him. It wasn't as if I could ring up directory enquiries and ask, "Can you put me through to the hangman please?" or even go into the local library and look in a Directory of Hangmen, was it?

Using my reporter's instinct and an idea of which part of the country I thought he lived in, I rang a local paper. The helpful person I spoke to gave me an address I could write to. I was full of optimism, but weeks went by without a reply. I even enclosed a stamped, addressed envelope.

Courtesy of the Royal Mail, my prayers, not that I had said any for years, were answered.

We arranged to meet and a fee was mentioned, which I have to say took me aback; I was not expecting to pay for any interview.

I travelled north and we met up. Seated in comfortable, leather armchairs in a smallish hotel, cups of tea asked for, we began. I was not exactly nervous but I must admit to being full of trepidation…

"In answer to your question, do I remember it? Yes, I remember it, nearly twenty years ago wasn't it?" he began.

Our interview was interrupted momentarily whilst the tea arrived. Bone china cups and saucers. I only ever used mugs at home and at the office.

We were surrounded by Victoriana, it was like being in a bit of a time warp, H.G. Wells' "The Time Machine", that's what it was, we had been sent back in time. It was a silly daydream, of course we hadn't.

"Can I take notes; it will be a lot quicker?" I asked.

"Fine by me", my guest replied.

"Was there anything special about it or him?"

"As far as I was concerned it was a job, there was nothing special about it or him if I recall. There was nothing special about any of them really, and I did a few, apart from one."

"Before we start could I ask you about the war crimes executions that you had a hand in?"

I was alluding to the aftermath of what had been the most infamous series of criminal trials ever held in the world. They were held in a small town in Germany, forever put on the map…Nuremberg.

He looked straight at me and took off his glasses, "No you can't."

"I'm sorry I hope I haven't upset you."

"You haven't but to be blunt, you are only paying me to hear about Jenkins, not about anything else, besides, it would take all day and I don't have the time."

I apologised sincerely and I meant it, although it would have been interesting.

"Could you continue telling me about the one you started to tell me about then?"

"I can, but it's nothing to do with this. But I will tell you, seeing as how I've started. It was during the war, in the Tower of London. A German spy who had been condemned to death. He tried to kill me, he had a good go as well, but he was held back. We half expected it, but did not think he would do anything silly. It took a while to calm him down though. A horrible person, between you and me. No time for spies, lowest of the low, especially whilst the war was on. I didn't take it personally though. If he had killed me someone else would have taken my place, but the job got done."

None of what he told me was said in a grandiose or boastful way. It was so matter of fact, so pragmatic.

It set the tone for what was to come.

Here I was taking tea with, without doubt, the most famous or infamous, depending on your point of view, hangman/executioner this country had ever had. He had opened the "trapdoor" to over four hundred people.

If any onlookers had been observing us we looked like a couple of businessman, with me taking shorthand notes of our conversation.

I knew how old he was, as if that had a bearing, he was seventy-five years old. He was certainly articulate, which would make my job a lot easier. Well turned out too, to use an Army analogy. A dark blue and white, thin pin striped, three-piece single breasted suit. A white shirt, navy tie and a pair of highly polished Oxford shoes. To the onlooker, if he or she existed other than in my imagination, he looked like a retired bank manager.

We finished the tea and I asked for some more. His story then began in earnest.

Chapter 51

"I ARRIVED on the train from Manchester to Leeds and got into a taxi outside the railway station, Leeds Central it was. I hadn't been to Leeds before, most of my work was in London. The taxi driver charged me a couple of bob, the cheeky bugger; it only took a few minutes."

"I got to the main gate at about 4 o'clock. I announced myself and was let in, the officer told me that I was expected, of course I was bloody expected, they could hardly do it without me could they? My assistant was already there. We didn't always work together but I had worked with him quite a few times. I liked the way he did things and we got on."

Here we were drinking tea, smoking cigarettes and talking about a workmate. It could have been any business, any profession, but the business we were discussing was the business of death.

The same waitress returned with a larger tea pot this time. I paid and we resumed...

He offered cigarettes from a silver coloured case. In any other line of work, this might have been a gift from a grateful client or customer, but not this one that was for sure.

"One of the governors arrived; we shook hands and exchanged pleasantries, as you did, then he led me into the prison proper, unlocking and locking gates in front and behind us. He had his own keys. I was shown to my quarters and shook hands with my assistant who was eating some toast. We talked about the job. We knew who he was and what he had been convicted of. It made no difference to us, it never did. He would be treated with as much deference and dealt with as professionally as anyone else.

"I never met him, didn't need to and never met any of them. All I needed to know was how tall he was, how much he weighed and what he had done for a living. I say that I never met them but I did see them, let me explain that.

"I did physically see him, I saw him whilst he was taking exercise in the yard, without him seeing me of course. That would have been too upsetting and might have made my job harder the next morning. If it hadn't been there I would have looked through the Judas Hole of the cell door. I had to in order to size him up so I could calculate the drop he would need. I had a chart, and still have it, a table of drops based on their height, their weight and whether or not they were manual workers."

He must have realised that I did not have the remotest idea what he was talking about by the look on my face and the fact that I had stopped writing to try to grasp his meaning.

"Sorry Max, the drop I am talking about, that I took for granted you knew about, is quite simply how long to make the rope itself. Too long and it could cause strangulation, too short and it could yank the head off. None of which is good. It has never happened with me thanks to my chart I am proud to say. The manual worker thing is if they do manual work the neck will be stronger. Does that explain it?"

I nodded; I was still in shock after visualising someone's head being yanked off.

He concluded this part by saying,

"Apart from the hemp rope, it was the most important tool in my box. As I said, it never let me down. My uncles started it off after some disasters many years ago."

It had slipped my mind that this had been a "family business".

After some talk of a general but not specific nature our waitress came back and asked if we might want some coffee this time. I asked my guest and he said that that he did. She emptied the by now overflowing ashtray and brought a clean one.

We now deviated to matters of a more domestic nature in the prison, and what happened in his quarters in particular.

"Every prison is different you know, with what they feed you. From memory, I think we had liver and onions for tea. They were exempt from rationing so I didn't have to use my ration card. He smiled as he said this, I didn't know whether he was being serious or not and I didn't ask him.

"I had a bottle of beer to wash it down with, just the one, we both did."

The coffee arrived, "Milk or cream?" she asked. I spoke for both of us and said, "Milk please".

"After tea we were told if he was out of his cell again."

"Why this time?" I asked

"So we could go next door to where he had been to stretch the rope overnight, it had a bag of sand attached to it that was the same weight as him. Setting it up made a bit of noise as we had to release the trapdoor to test that as well."

I was truly mesmerised, hanging, please forgive the pun onto his every word.

"And next door was?"

As soon as I asked the question, I knew the answer to it.

"Sorry, forget that, I know where you mean."

"Once that was done we went back to our quarters and usually had a game of cards, not for money, just for matchsticks," he laughed aloud. "A mug of cocoa and then lights out at about half past nine. The beds in Leeds were like ex-Army bunks, horsehair mattresses." I knew exactly what he meant and said so. "And no, before you ask, I never had any trouble sleeping."

I paused to sharpen my pencil, emptying the shavings from my penknife into the ashtray. He was full of it and seemed to be enjoying telling me this, or at least I hoped he was.

"We were woken up from our separate rooms at about six o'clock the next morning. Washed, shaved and I wore the same suit I had travelled in. Burtons, off the peg, three-piece and single breasted. I still have it. I always favoured three-piece suits; they looked more business-like, white shirt and a black tie. It was a routine, a ritual if you like, my uniform.

We had breakfast; I didn't wear my jacket to eat that though. Didn't want any egg dripping down it did I? We had a natural pause whilst he went to use the toilet. In his temporary absence, I poured out some more of the distinctly average coffee.

Chapter 52

"BREAKFAST over and done with it was time to concentrate on the matter in hand. We were shown up to the landing and took our shoes off. We wanted to be as quiet as mice so as not to make him aware that we were even there. The rope was pulled up and put in position over the scaffold itself with the knot in place. We were ready in plenty of time, we always were. Nothing was left to chance. We went for a pot of tea at the end of this landing, as I recall."

"The governor appeared then, not the one we had met yesterday, the real one. I don't say that out of any disrespect, but it was his prison after all. He told us there would be no last minute reprieve and the execution would go ahead as planned."

That pleased me, as it meant I would be paid the full amount. I was the senior man and I got more than my assistant, that is how it worked. If It had been cancelled we would have got nothing apart from travelling expenses.

My goodness, I thought, he was careful about money. He had mentioned it an awful lot. Why not though? It was a skill that few other people ever had and he should be remunerated for it. It was in that respect like listening to a tradesman, very incongruous.

We lit up again, at the rate of cigarettes we were going through his petrol lighter would need refilling.

"Just before what I used to refer to as the appointed hour, 9 o'clock in this case as it usually was, the whole entourage", what a lovely word that is I thought.

"The governor, the High Sheriff, the deputy governor and two officers appeared in the corridor. The landing had coconut matting on a long length of it to deaden the sound of their footsteps. The prison chaplain was already inside. The governor looked at his watch and nodded to me, it was time. The door fully opened, we, my assistant and I, went in straight after him. The rest stayed outside for the time being. The two officers who had been outside walked with a purpose past us and moved the wardrobe to one side that led to the chamber."

"Could Jenkins have seen this, seen the noose?" I asked.

"It depends on which way he was looking but I imagine so, he turned round to see the wardrobe being shifted. I looked at him as he sat on his chair and he stood up, almost to attention. He had been expecting me, or someone like me, for a while. I seem to recall that a smile came onto his face. This was not a social meeting although I remember reading in one of the papers that he had always wanted to meet me. Whether or not that was just "paper talk" he got his wish all right."

I did not know what to expect next, although I had an idea. This was a blow-by-blow account of an execution, an actual execution, described by the man who carried it out.

"My assistant stood at his back, took hold of his arms and fastened the leather strap around his wrists with his arms pinioned at the back. Tight enough to prevent his arms from flaying out."

"Follow me," I said to him and he did as I asked, they always did. My mate held his shoulders as he was put on the trap door and put a strap around his ankles to stop his legs from coming apart as I whipped out what looked like a white handkerchief from my top pocket. It was a hood and it went over his head. "Clear the drop," was what I said next. My assistant took out the cotter pin holding the lever in place, which I then pushed forward, the trapdoors sprung open and gravity did the rest."

How long did this take, you know, the whole thing?"

"Usually ten to twelve seconds, we were always on the clock. I was told that I did one once in eight seconds."

"Bloody hell, eight seconds?" I blurted out.

"I think that was only the once and don't ask me who or where it was because I couldn't tell you if I tried to."

I was still thinking, daydreaming again, about the trapdoor and my mind wandered to the person who had made it. It had no other purpose did it? What was the occupation of the person who made it? Did he have a business card stating he was "An execution trapdoor maker?" Without being prompted, something I never had to do with him, he continued.

"We left the body where it was for a good half an hour, but the prison doctor had already been into the pit below to certify death. We then did the final bit, lowered the body and put him onto a gurney. We took his clothes off and put a shroud over him. The body was then taken away for a post mortem."

"I didn't realise that," I said.

"Oh yes that had to be done. They couldn't bury him without a death certificate and there had to be a post mortem to show what he died of."

"What did that say?"

"Death by judicial hanging, fracture of the second vertebrae, to be precise. It's also to show that I have done my job properly. I didn't want to be criticised for doing a botched job and I never was. It is all recorded in a book at the prison and they send a copy to my bosses at the Home Office."

My guest then took out his pocket watch attached to a gold Albert chain in his waistcoat. "Time's up I'm afraid, I've got to be going. Could you order me a taxi to the railway station please?"

The inside pocket of my suit jacket contained a white paper envelope that had in it £25 guineas in cash, not a brown envelope, plus his travelling expense of £2.17 shillings. It was hard, if not impossible, to quantify how much the going rate was to interview a hangman. But he had told me in advance.

As we took our leave of each other and shook hands, the hands that had despatched hundreds into eternity, outside the hotel he looked up at the sign and said, "Funny name for a hotel in Harrogate that."

He pointed to the name of the hotel, the Hotel Isola Bella, where our meeting had taken place. My impish sense of humour has never deserted me and anyway, it was my turn to be ironic, where else would we have met?

EXTRACTS FROM THE NEWS
OF THE WORLD

IT WAS DESCRIBED as "Amazing and exclusive memoirs". The by-line read "by one who knew him".

I never did find out who this person was…

"Not for the first time Nicholas Jenkins celebrates a birthday in prison this morning. He is 40 today. The man found guilty at Leeds Assizes of the murder of Mrs Amelia Sanders, the 69 year old widow, has been confined at Leeds Prison ever since.

"However from what Jenkins has said we will try to paint a picture of the man with whom the public is not yet familiar. The facts should be told and they can only be told through this newspaper.

"There is little doubt Jenkins is a man of near genius, a man of musical and financial flair. His contemporaries say that he could have been a millionaire before he reached the age he is now.

"That is one picture. But there is also another side to this man which The News of the World intends to place before its readers. This other side of this astonishing man will amaze and probably shock the world.

"The last time he was exposed to the public gaze he was immaculately dressed, not a hair out of place, shoes perfectly polished. Today he wears the jacket, shirt and trousers issued to men condemned to die. A man in the shadow of the noose.

"When, for the last time, he stepped from the dock at Leeds Assizes he had a half smile, almost sardonic, on his lips. As most of our readers will be aware, apart from saying "Nothing at all" when he was sentenced and "not guilty my Lord" to the judge when asked how he pleaded at the start of the trial, he never said anything else throughout the proceedings. There was no emotion as he went to the cells beneath the court.

"This quite amazing character, found guilty of the most ghastly crimes, could also sit in his cell and write letters to his aged parents amongst others. To his mother and father he would sign them, "ever your loving Sonnie". It was a term of affection that he used throughout the letters to his parents. They addressed him as Nicholas.

He would talk in these letters about the weather, the government and mention that for security reasons he couldn't tell them about what he did on a daily basis. In particular he tried to make light of the fact that he was not allowed to tell them what time he took exercise as the authorities were scared that his parents would have a car with its engine running outside the prison walls ready to facilitate his escape!

In one of his earlier letters, after his committal to the assizes, he wrote,

"I found the hearing quite amusing, it all seemed so unreal, like watching a badly written play for the second time thinking that it couldn't be as bad again. Am not the least bit worried, why should I worry?"

His arrogance continued to shine through, "It will be a

big case: in fact I should think it will be the biggest case in British history.

"My guards tell me that I am the talk of the prison."

The News of the World continued…

"There were as many sides to his nature as there are facets in a brilliant cut diamond.

"We have observed his appearance, his neat and regular features. Even whilst on remand he had a regular visit from his barber who travelled from Harrogate at a cost of 2 guineas a time. His wardrobe was extensive and varied, there were clothes for all occasions.

"He preferred a dozen suits to last for twelve years rather than to last a year, handmade in Savile Row as were his shirts. A selection of neckties in various shades of red, his favourite colour. Old school ties, club and regimental ties, none of which he either went to, belonged to or served in to be awarded the accord of being able to wear them legitimately.

"He had an obsession with cleanliness and wore gloves the whole year round. He would never touch a piano keyboard or pick up a book if it looked dirty. Then there were the cars, he was obsessed with them, fast, well-maintained cars, cars to impress others with his last one being an Alvis coupe costing almost £1500

"As his barrister at his trial revealed, Jenkins was brought up in a strict Plymouth Brethren home. What the average child regarded as pleasures he knew nothing of. Not for him the celebration of birthdays and Christmas. He was not able to dance even. His main social skill was playing the piano and listening to classical music. He never used bad language or profanities.

"He drank sparingly although never a particular lover of beer. So one of the many questions remains, what else did he do with the money that he made? The answer, as far as this paper has been able to gather, is that he was an inveterate gambler. Bookmakers seemed to be the main beneficiaries of his ill-gotten gains.

"He could have been a successful inventor, albeit self-taught. He had lots of good ideas but they came to naught and so he turned to crime. After his dalliances with petty crimes he graduated with honours from his last prison. He used his skills as a con man, a forger and eventually a murderer, a murderer like no other."

In typical News of the World style the paper carried the headline…

"The Last Hours of a Condemned Man"

Although the paper had relegated the story to page 5 it had done its job with the circulation up to approximately 8 million copies per week. An increase of two million readers! One for every six people in the United Kingdom!

"Nicholas Jenkins went to the gallows with the familiar half smile on his face. Precisely what his innermost feelings were as he walked the short distance to his death and to meet the hangman will never be known. A friend who visited him said that he looked well. His appearance was far from displeasing although his hair was dry and his eyes were tired from reading and writing his last letters.

"One thing that was said to have concerned him greatly however, and which illustrates his intense vanity and complete detachment from his fate, was that those people who looked at his effigy in Madame Tussauds would be looking at him. Correct in every detail, even down to the shirt cuff being half an inch below his suit jacket cuff. Since going on display in the Chamber of Horrors, two days after he was judicially executed, hundreds of people have queued along Marylebone Road, paying their admission money and gazing at him as well as the others in there. As far as notorious murderers are concerned, Jenkins is in good company."

For the News of the World and indeed Madame Tussauds, there is no bigger business than the business of death.

The victims of these murders seem to be forgotten about, almost superfluous in fact. As the "Bard of Stratford" said, "Twas ever thus."

Ironically, without them Jenkins would never have achieved the longer lasting notoriety he has achieved.

EPILOGUE

When Jenkins was arrested, it was if a 2000 piece jigsaw had been thrown up in the air. Some of the pieces landed face up, some landed face down, and indeed some were missing and would never be found. The puzzle had to be completed to make sense of all of this.

Many people in diverse occupations and professions played a part in its completion. The Police, forensic pathologists, barristers, hotel owners and the relatives of their guests, and many, many more.

Nevertheless, the only person who actually met him, and knew him for years outside of any legal context, was my cousin Veronica. I felt sure that we would never see each other again but I would be eternally grateful to her, more than she would ever know.

Jenkins was many things, a paradox, a monster and an enigma even. I had never read anything like this and I never will again. He talked about killing people as a business, which to him it was. He knew that it was wrong to kill people and to dispose of them in the way that he did. He didn't care.

The only things that he seemed to care about were his friendship with Veronica, his appearance and the fact that he had been caught. I formed the impression that he would have kept on killing. Taking innocent lives just because they had what he wanted.

In the final analysis I and anyone else reading this only had his word, the word of a pathological liar, a psychopathic killer, that what he was saying through this manuscript was the truth. Had he been "brainwashed" by his parents at an early age? Did this religious mania almost have an effect on his formative years? Or was he just a common criminal?

I don't know the answers and never will.

Was it the truth as he saw it?

Had I, by reading this, been manipulated by him just like his victims?

Was I "Judy" to his "Mr Punch", did he have me dancing on a string like a puppet?

Even in the condemned cell, he was always in control, or so he thought, but at the end, the very end, someone else took control of his life and turned it into death, his death.

Now that was true irony.

Who was the marionette now, Mr Nicholas Jenkins?

Not me; I wasn't the one hanging from a rope was I?

ACKNOWLEDGMENTS

To Tony Hutchinson, "Hutch" for his help, advice and friendship which has been invaluable.

To Paul Stickler, for believing that this could become a reality.

To Les Stead, for his brilliant original artwork and to Eddie Burton for allowing me to use his name. Two good detectives and good people.

And finally:

To all the many people who have helped me with the research I think this book warranted and deserved. Everybody has been so helpful and I am indebted to them.

Thank you...